LUMINESCENCE

A LUMINESENCE NOVEL

BOOK 1

By

J.L. Weil

D0981580

Published by Nevermore Press

Fort Wayne, IN 46804. 2014

Text Copyright © 2014 J.L. Weil

All Rights Reserved

This book is a work of fiction. Names, characters, businesses, organizations, places, events, and incidents either are the product of the author's imagination or are used fictitiously. Any resemblance to actual persons, living or dead, events, or locales is entirely coincidental.

This book is sold subject to the condition that it shall not, by way of trade or otherwise, be lent, re-sold, duplicated, hired out, or otherwise circulated without the publisher's prior written consent in any form of binding or cover other than that in which it is published and without similar condition including this condition being imposed on the subsequent purchaser.

Copyright © 2014 Nevermore Press

All rights reserved

Published by

Nevermore Press.

Fort Wayne, IN 46804

Edited by: Dawn White

For Nevermore Press

Formatting by: Nevermore Press

www.NevermorePress.com

CHAPTER 1

I WAS PISSED – SERIOUSLY PISSED.

And that only meant extreme trouble. Enough, that even in my heightened anger, I was frightened. Scared not for myself but for anyone who got in the path of the fury just past my control.

The ripple of heat flowed through my veins – bubbled to boiling point. It scorched my skin, causing a line of crimson haze to swivel in front of my eyes. So hot it felt like the flames from a dragon licked at the back of my throat, threatening to lash from my mouth if I dared speak. Clamping my teeth together excruciatingly, I avoided my lips in the process. The thought of tasting my own blood didn't bode well at this very moment. Not with the intense tingle I felt everywhere.

"Let it go Brianna." I faintly heard Austin's resigned voice. He might have touched a hand to my arm, but I was too far in depths for reasoning.

Early on, I learned that my temper was something to avoid at all costs – all costs. I went to severe pains to keep it under wrap. Deep breathing and the whole find your center of balance thing. I'd taken classes in mediation. Learning to control my emotions, doing what I could to protect others from myself. It had been so long since it had hit me with such intensity that I had forgotten what it was like, had forgotten that it was wrong.

Experimenting with my odd, peculiar and volatile temper was something I never did. Trying to pick it apart and find out the particulars to why it initiated such bizarre and often harmful results didn't sound like a good idea. The sensations it induced made me feel out-of-control, wild, and reckless. Like there was nothing, and no one that could stand in my way. I felt empowered. Then after I'd seen the results of what I'd done, I was consumed with guilt and shame. A freak. What normal person inflicts the impossible with just a flare of anger?

Usually it wasn't an issue. I made sure of it. Keeping mostly to myself, I had just a few close friends. Even they didn't know the violence that lived within – no one knew. Not my friends, not my parents when they were alive, and not even the one person I trusted and loved most in this world – my aunt.

Part of it was shame and part of it was fear. What if someone found out? I'd no doubt be branded as the freak I felt. The nuthouse would be my new home.

None of it made sense, which was why I don't stress about it.

Normally.

Regardless, I tried not to reflect about my freakish attribute, and how different it made me. What I wouldn't give to be free of whatever curse or hex I'd been born with. That was how I thought of it. A curse. Nothing like this could be good. Mostly I refused to allow myself to get mad or on the verge of angry. I walked away.

Until today.

I would have today if only Rianne had let it go. If she hadn't pushed me further and further until there was no other response but to react. If only she hadn't chosen this day to harass and bully one of my best friends. And maybe if I hadn't already been in a shitty mood from the day of hell I was already having. There had been an underlying headache that just wouldn't quit, gnawing away at the back of my skull. Or if Tori, Austin and I had stayed another minute at our locker's fooling around we wouldn't have passed Rianne in the hollow.

But as it turned out, we did pass by Rianne, and she *had* bumped purposely into Austin knocking him downing, spewing vile words at him in her cheerleading skanky voice. A voice which begged me to tear her into shreds and rip out her wicked tongue, she had no regard for the hurt she caused others.

Austin wasn't a big guy. He might have a few feet over my five-foot, two-inch frame, putting him almost at equal level with Rianne. His weight wasn't much better, which hardly made sense since he ate like a dying horse on its last meal. Today he had on skinny jeans, emphasizing his scrawny legs. Hair, product styled, still perfectly in place, framed by his bottle glass green eyes now crystal and bright with humiliation. He had the whole GQ thing going for him.

Nonetheless, it wasn't how Austin looked or how he dressed that had Rianne yelling those choice words out over the hollow. It wasn't enough that she'd purposely rammed into him while we were making our way through the crowd. If it had been anything else, I would have been able to maintain the thread holding my anger in check.

"Get out of the way faggot." She shrieked over the bustle and commotion of the circular room as kids made their way to final period. With both palms spread, she took advantage of his unsteadiness and shoved, sprawling him over the mascot in the center where practically the entire school congregated between classes.

Yep, Austin was gay.

My control snapped like a rubber band. The combination of hearing my friend being called that ugly name, and seeing him tossed ass first on the schools dull gray carpet, I felt the first inklings of my temper peak.

Momentarily stunned I just glared at Rianne while the

assault of emotions snuck up on me. Somewhere in the smog I remembered Tori speaking to Austin.

"You okay?" she whispered, giving Austin a hand up.

If he had given her a reply it was lost by the bursting flood of rage that had consumed me.

Recklessly, I reached out in front of me and grabbed Rianne's arm, stopping her from turning and walking away. Her sneering golden eyes pierced into mine with disgust, like little spears of hate. She couldn't believe that I had the gall to touch her. I was normally quiet and very non-confrontational. This was so out of the norm it hit a home run off left field.

With a tug she attempted to shake off my grasp, but my hold held like a vise grip. "L-E-T go of me," she hissed through clenched teeth, drawing out the threat. But her anger was nothing to match my own. Right then my fury spiked. I felt the fervor racing in my blood and tumbling into my fingertips. My hand trembled under the tight clutch I had on her arm.

When I spoke, my voice sounded nothing like my own. It quivered with potency. "Like hell. You should watch what you say," I spat.

There was a falter in her expression when I realized she'd felt the burn, the sting that radiated from my fingers. Again she tried to wiggle out of my hold. When she failed a second time, her gaze turned to mine and widened in astonishment, skepticism and a touch of fear.

"Your eyes," she accused, staring intently into mine. "What's wrong with your eyes?" her voice cracked, giving away the incredulity and dubiety she must have felt. Appalled, her feet scrambled to back-up.

Stepping forward, my heart accelerated. Thumping heavily against my chest, her admission put anxiety into my stomach. I let go of her arm with a quick jerk. She stumbled once, unsteady on her feet but never took her eyes from mine. They bore into me with fear, repulsion and disbelief, branding me like the freak I felt.

My breath came in quick pants as I averted my gaze and closed my eyes tight, trying to get a handle on the rage still pumping in me. Calming the quick pants to longer slower ones, I recalled one of the meditation techniques I'd learned. I didn't know what Rianne thought she saw in my eyes other than extreme anger, I tried to cajole. Even if her fear had been real, it was hardly past Rianne's character to make a fool out of others in front of the whole school. Hell, it was what she did on a daily basis.

Continuing to mentally talk myself down, I felt the slow recession of my flare-up. The warmth faded from my skin, and the overwhelming urge to punish Rianne drifted with the loss of contact.

"Brianna, are you okay?" I heard Tori ask behind me over the swiftly receding roar in my skull.

Shaking my head I tried to clear the rattled outburst, berating myself for the enormous slip in front of the entire school nonetheless. If I wasn't thought of as odd and weird before, this just put me on the front page of weirdo's attending Holly Ridge High.

"What did you do to me?" Rianne screeched accusingly at me in a tone of contempt and outrage.

Saying nothing, I opened my eyes to see her clutching the arm I had grasped. Dread sunk to the soles of my converse covered heels. Had I really done that? Was I capable of inflicting that kind of harm with just my fingers?

Bright, swollen cherry marks lined Rianne's arm in the spots my fingers had clasped. The wound looked like imprints or burn marks from a flatiron that had penetrated her flesh, except my fingers had been the branding iron.

There was no doubt of the horror I saw now blistering Rianne's forearm. Embarrassment, regret and shame swarmed my gut, twisting it heavily with sour guilt. Not willing to answer questions I didn't have answers for, I quickly turned to leave.

Like a gust of wind I became acutely aware of the large audience my spectacle had created. They stood circled around

Rianne, Tori, Austin and I, some chanting and jeering our names, encouraging a fight.

Without a second thought I pushed my way through an opening in the awkward sea of people. Rushing before someone could stop me or prior to teacher arrival, the need for escape steamrolled over me.

There were too many eyes.

Too many questions.

Too much emotion.

My mind seemed to have temporarily abandoned me. There was no other explanation for my actions, or for my legs carrying me not to my last class but to the exit doors of the school. I'd never in three years of high school ever ditched out on a class.

I know, unfathomable.

However, I'm among the select few who like school. Okay maybe not so much school but learning. Being shy and mostly socially challenged, books were more my friend than my peers – Tori and Austin the exception.

My actions today were so out of character for me, I began to doubt who I thought I was. I hated confrontation. I never caused trouble. And I don't attack people in the hall, burning the fuse on my temper.

Never.

Right now all I knew was that I had to get out of here, run from what I had just done.+. The walls of the school suffocated me in their confines.

As I stepped out the front door of school, a soothing breeze whipped through my tousled dark hair. Washing over the flush in my face, it cooled the heat that had crept up on me during my impermissible mood. The balmy air was scented with just a taste of the ocean in the distance, it never seemed far away.

Holly Ridge, North Carolina had been in the midst of one of those dreamy sun-drenched days. But now gray clouds were rolling across the sky. The ground was drenched from a downpour of rain. A crackling of lightning lit in the distance followed by a gentle rumble of thunder. Whatever storm had passed through was on its way out. Ironic that it fit my mood. Dreary and unpredictable.

Peering around at the lush landscape, a sight I often took for granted, the overhang of trees and grass met the sandy shores, and then plunged into depths of expansive turquoise sparkling sea. The grass began to glisten as sunbeams tried to break through the storm clouds.

Inhaling a deep gush of flavored misty air, I rounded the corner to the backside of the building, rushing toward the parking lot. A strange prickly sensation climbed over me, like clashing with a cactus. Doing my best to brush it off, I took the corner faster than planned and sped up my retreat. Unfortunately I wasn't the only one who apparently skipped out of school early today.

Leaning comfortably against the wall was an unfamiliar face, and in my haste I smacked into him. Literally. My face connected with the solid front of his chest, hands clutching on the muscle of his biceps. In an impossible gut-reaction he caught me in his arms. We wavered a tad, but he managed to keep us erect instead of mortifying me further and tumbling us to the grass.

Damn, I thought. What else could happen today?

I forced my glance upwards from the black cotton tee that conformed to his chest, ready to apologize for my clumsiness. Heedless of how much I wanted to keep my head lowered, I would rather run and forget this day happened. His hands tingled on my arms still holding me. It should have been too intimate for comfort, but I found the opposite to be true. A sense of safety came over me, probably because he had just saved me from falling all over him.

My hands released their grip and flattened on his chest. His heart quickened under my fingers. The scent of him drifted to my senses smelling of the forest, wild and reckless. The apology I'd been about to utter got stuck in the back of my throat. In that blinding moment I tripped into a set of sapphire eyes. My own heart picked up speed, thumping wildly in my chest – uncontainable like stallions roaming the plains. Nothing like the trepidation I felt previously. This was racing excitement.

He raised a perfectly arched brow decorated with a studded bar. His eyes sparkled with amusement, assumingly at my gaping stare. I was on the other hand, unaware that I'd stood stunned, feet planted with no attempt to move from his arms. In retrospect, I can only hope he didn't find me as stupid as I later felt.

My gaze wandered from his eyes down the planes of his cheeks, to lips donned with yet another piercing. This one was a hoop in the center of his lower lip. Those silver studded lips upturned into a lazy smirk. I watched fascinated by the curl of his mouth. An intense string of butterflies flew in my stomach. They felt more like fireflies because of the warmth that swirled with the exhilaration. Fleetingly, I wondered if there were any more parts of him pierced.

His mouth lowered the tiniest fraction closer to mine. The breath I held caught in what I never would have imagined – anticipation. I actually wanted this strange guy to press his lips to mine. Right now it was all I wanted – his kiss. The zeal of his breath fanned my senses, making me dizzy with the scent of him. My mind must have taken a detour between eighth and ninth period.

A gentle stroke of his thumb on my bare arm sent a shudder down my spine, knocking me out of my spellbound gape. I jerked out of his embrace, immediately missing the contact. What was wrong with me? I don't encourage strange guys to kiss me, really any guy for that matter.

"What are you doing?" I demanded harsher than intended.

He arched his pierced brow again mockingly. "Saving you it seems. Obviously I'm not the only one ditching last period."

His voice was an extension of his look. Dark. Sexy. Edgy. Mysterious. And don't forget Dangerous.

Not precisely the kind of guy you'd want to meet alone in an alley, bring home to mom or behind the school yard for that matter.

He was dressed from head to toe in black, dark denim with a loud t-shirt, combat boots and a thick leather band around his wrist. This guy wasn't shy about jewelry. He had a James Dean quality, rebel without a cause ambiance.

Now that I wasn't so enamored by his eyes I could appreciate the whole package. His hair was layered around his face with flirtatious slashing strands black as sin. He was a mouth full of eye candy. Yummy and delicious.

"I – I don't normally ditch class," I stammered, running a frustrated hand through my tangled hair.

The look he gave said he found me entertaining, but didn't buy into the whole not ditching thing. He just shrugged his shoulders.

Narrowing my eyes at him I slung the bag that had slipped back over my shoulder. "I've never seen you before. Do you even go here?"

His eyes caught mine again, and they seemed to laugh. "Umm yeah – It's my first day."

"You ditched on your first day?" My voice sounded as perplexed as the idea was to me.

"Sure. It seems worth it now." His voice held sex appeal. Husky and dark. "I'm Gavin," he introduced, shoving both hands in his pockets now that he wasn't holding onto me.

"Brianna," I replied. The last warning bell sounded reminding me that I shouldn't be loitering. "I should go," I mumbled hastily.

He leaned back casually against the brick wall, one leg propped up behind him. "I'll be seeing you Bri." He shortened my name like we were acquainted more than we were. His husky voice held promise.

I couldn't tell if I was flattered or insulted. "Sorry

about… running into you," I uttered and turned toward the parking lot not waiting for a response. I couldn't get to my car fast enough.

When I got inside my aging mustang, I wasn't sure what to do next or where to go. Everything inside me was muddled. An inability to get a handle on the rattled emotions overcame me. The lingering exhaustion from my anger slowly started dissipating and was now accompanied by the bursting excitement in my chest. All of it was too much. The need to unwind and smooth my frazzled nerves was too great to ignore. The first thing that came to mind was my aunt and her shop, *Mystic Floral and Gifts.*

CHAPTER 2

MY AUNT WAS LIKE NO OTHER – she was amazing. Her small floral boutique was located in the heart of downtown Holly Ridge, my part-time job. The short ride from school had done little for my frayed emotions. I felt like I had just been bungee jumping, flying from pissed off to shame – a giant drop. Then to a confused excitement that if I didn't know better resembled attraction. This Gavin wasn't my type, not that I really had a type. You would've had to of dated. My inabilities to find a niche in life were no doubt contributing factors.

My aunt's shop was enchanting and potent. The second you walked in you were dazzled with the serene smells of lilies, lavender and freesia. She has this impressive window display that captivated people, encouraging them in, showing off her flair for the dramatic. Cornflower velvet draped over stands of various heights, her floral arrangements cascading over like green waterfalls, clusters of rainbow crystals sparkling like magic in the morning sun.

I've always had a complete ease and sense of belonging here. The atmosphere she created was what I identified with. Otherworldly. Fantasy. An escape from reality.

Right now I needed all of the above.

Walking into the shop I noticed my aunt behind the glass counter with a customer. Her silky long caramel hair lay softly over her shoulders. Such a contrast to my own dark strands. Her smooth and creamy skin shone flawlessly against the sunbeams from the storefront windows and soft mahogany eyes twinkling.

My Aunt Clara is my legal guardian. She and my mom had been twins. Sometimes it was peculiar having my aunt look and sound like an exact duplicate of my mom. When I was younger it had been much more difficult.

At age five I came to live with my Aunt Clara here at her home. I was orphaned after a drunk driver killed both my parents on New Year's Eve. Gwynn and Andrew Rafferty had been on their way home from a business event with my dad's firm when the tragic accident occurred. I don't have clear memories of that day, only a snapshot in my head of the way they were elegantly dressed, and the smell of her perfume, like roses as she hugged me good-bye.

I do remember the empty confusion after the fact. My aunt cried with me through our pain, kissed the salty tears from my eyes, and held onto me at night when I was frightened and alone. She became my rock.

Even now, years later, when I caught the scent of a rose

in full bloom, I would ache. And wonder what life would have been. The what if game… I detested playing those wishing games. The loss of my parents wasn't something I reflected on often. Although, it snuck up on me and squeezed the place that they hold in a corner of my heart.

Mostly I deluded myself into believing that I was nothing but an average teenager. After today, my doubts skyrocketed. What I needed was confirmation that I wasn't an oddity or needed to be locked up in the loony bin. Maybe I did need therapy. But right now I wanted my aunt.

Passing by one of the mirrors used on display, I caught a glimpse of my reflection. A loud sigh escaped my lips. How I yearned for the elegant grace and classic beauty of my mom and aunt. In truth, there were none of those traits within me. Instead I was graced with unmanageable auburn hair. My skin was anything but flawless, maybe it would have passed for adequate if not for the dusting of freckles over the bridge of my dainty nose. I scrunched it in the reflection just to prove my point.

My aunt said I have a unique look. What does that mean? Does she mean unique as in appealing or unique as in odd? Probably she was just trying to keep my self-esteem from reaching an all-time low. I had a hard time looking at myself and visualizing anything uncommon. Just the same face. The one I've seen for the last seventeen years.

Ordinary.

I'll admit I did have an odd feature. One I guessed you could call *novel* – my eyes. They are a profound violet, like an amethyst.

Strolling around the shop I trailed a finger along the shelves, trying anything to distract my mind. *Mystic Floral* was my aunt's heart and soul. She was divorced, and I think the store had become her saving grace. Being the owner did take an exuberate amount of her time. She often felt guilty that I spent much of it alone and taking care of myself. When I was younger I would spend my afternoons in the shop until closing. This place had been as much of home as the house on Mulberry.

I admired my aunt's gift with plants, and her artistic design to make something beautiful. It was in this place I could breathe. The smells were so alive and aromatic, the environment spellbinding. I traced my nail along some of the new colored decorative bottles she had arranged glistening against crystal stones.

"Brianna." Her voice was like a warm hearth, filled with security. I turned to face her. "You're early, is everything okay?" She checked the time on her wrist.

Swallowing hard I didn't know whether to cry, laugh,

or hug her. Instead I lied, something that I don't do very well. "I got sick before last period." I kept my eyes averted to the tiled floor, and silently prayed she wouldn't see through my ruse.

She pursed her lips looking concerned. "Why don't you go home and take the night off. You look a little... peaked." Her caring suggestion only made me feel more guilty than I thought possible.

"It's not as bad now," I assured. "Would it be all right if I stayed?" I asked hesitantly. I really wanted her company, the calm reassurance of love.

"Yeah honey, if that's what you want." She totally didn't buy my flimsy excuse, but I knew she wouldn't hound me until I was ready to talk.

I nodded my head.

"Why don't you help me set out some of these arrangements I just finished." She encouraged knowing that I needed anything to help ease my mind.

An hour into my shift I headed to the backroom in hopes of occupying my thoughts with homework. Mister dark and dangerous seemed to find a way to flitter his way into my head. The shop had a bell on the door that chimed at the arrival of a customer.

I found my aunt sitting at her work table crafting a

display with flowers my untrained eyes have yet to be able identify. She cut the ends on their long stems. "Feeling any better?" Concern fed her tone.

I took a seat beside her, picking up the discarded stems. "Some." Surprisingly, it was true.

"Good. You want to talk about it?" She could tell that something was bothering me. I sucked at hiding my emotions. And lying.

I sighed. "I just had a horrible day." Horrific was more like it. "I had a headache that wouldn't quit. Then a girl at school was bullying Austin and –" I paused, not sure how to tell her.

"Did you say something to this girl?" She clipped another stem from a pretty blush colored flower.

"I kind of grabbed her arm. Hard." Admitting it was tougher than I expected, and I kept my eyes locked onto the grain of the table.

She put the flower down and eyed me. "Did it go further than that?" she asked probably wondering if we'd exchanged blows in the halls. The whole hair pulling and nail scratching deal or if she was going to be getting a call from the principal.

I shook my head, lifting my gaze. "I left school right after and came here. I wanted to punish her for all the crap she's been giving Austin, but I didn't want to physically hurt her." Well if I was being honest with myself, at the time it was exactly what I wanted to do. Reflexively I brushed a strand of stray hair behind by ear.

She eyed me with worry. "I know it's challenging, dealing with those who have no care for others feelings. You did nothing wrong by defending your friend."

Then why did I have so much guilt? I knew that she was trying to pacify my inner turmoil, but I wasn't sure there was anything she could say that would absorb it from me.

"I know that in my head but it's my conscious that doesn't agree. I feel like I lost myself somewhere during the day. Like my control just snapped," I begrudgingly admitted and slumped in my seat.

"What happened may be uncharacteristic for you, but everyone has a breaking point. Maybe you found yours." She gathered the fresh cut flowers and began piecing them into a crystal vase.

"Yeah, I guess." I was unconvinced.

Pushing the abundant flower filled vase aside, she faced me. "You have always had a soft heart. It's something to be proud of."

Her words recalled a memory of me at nine caring for a weakened baby bunny lost from its family. Immediately I took

25

it in, swaddled it in blankets and feed it baby formula with an eye dropper. For weeks I doted on this tiny bunny, afraid he wasn't going to be strong enough on his own, willing with all my might that he would survive. He did. The day I released him back into the trees bordering my yard was a mixture of gratified happiness and an achy sorrow, but I knew he was going to thrive.

"You're right." I attempted a half smile for her sake. Propping my elbows on the table, I placed my chin in my hands and exhaled. "Now all I have to deal with is the gossip tomorrow."

"You're stronger than you can imagine," she said as she engulfed me in hug filled with unconditional love. Her hair brushed against my cheek and smelled of lilacs. Leaning my head on her shoulder, I took a moment to appreciate what she meant to me.

By the time my shift ended at the shop I was physically spent. I pulled up into our driveway, and my eyes roamed over the house of all my childhood memories. The two-story pearly white colonial trimmed in black. A veranda swept off both sides of the house. In the center of the front view was a massive cobblestone fireplace. Here and there the cobblestone was accented throughout. My aunt of course landscaped the yard, looking like something out of *Better Homes and*

Gardens.

My favorite part of the house has always been the large pear tree that sat off the garage. I loved when the tree blossomed in the spring, stuffing its branches with the white flowers. The sheen petals forever ended up dusted over the yard. My aunt inherited the house from my Grandma when she declared there was too much unused space for just her. She wanted something low-key and less work, a maintenance free townhome. The house had been a part of our family for generations. It was very old but well kept.

Walking inside I headed to the kitchen. The house was quiet and creaked in certain spots underfoot. There were some leftovers from last night that I had planned on having for dinner but my stomach was still unsettled from the day's events. Grabbing a can of coke from the fridge, I headed upstairs to my room.

Moving out of habit, I changed my clothes and discarded the old ones in the hamper. By nature I was neat and liked things in order. Going to the window, I cracked it, letting the twilight breeze into my room, cooling the humidity. I pulled back the covers, fluffed my pillow and climbed into bed.

That night I found the restlessness had returned, and I was unable to sleep in spite of being exhausted. My mind raced with images, darting from Rianne to Gavin and back to Rianne.

27

What had happened to me today? I didn't even recognize myself.

Fighting.

Ditching class.

Engaging with a trouble maker.

Wanting to kiss the trouble maker.

I covered my hands over my face with mortification at just the thought of how I'd acted. I was a basket case.

Snippets of Rianne's cherry rash on her arm, and the terror and accusation in her face kept me up. My mind over exaggerated the incident. There had to be a rational explanation of what I'd done and more importantly, how. So I grabbed her arm, but tight enough to leave marks like that? It was the only plausible solution my mind could come up with and nowhere near made me feel better.

Eventually in the late hours of the night, my body relinquished to the rest it sought. My dreams however, were anything but peaceful.

CHAPTER 3

THE DREAM WAS ONE I had many times before. Maybe not the same dream per se but always of him. The blond haired boy with emerald eyes which beckoned me.

Lukas Devine.

He was as *divine* as his name indicated. He looked like the boy next door, clean cut, athletic built and a charming smile. The random dreams of him have existed since I can remember. They had become such a part of my sleep that I welcomed his arrival.

The fact that I converse with a hot guy in my dreams was just another sad page of my so called life. He had been the most exciting part, gloomy I know, until my run-in with Gavin. I chopped it up to being stuff dreams were made of. Perhaps that feeling only existed in the fantasy my mind created. Other than this made-up guy of my dreams, no one had come close to making me feel the heat rushed exhilaration that I'd experienced with Gavin.

The dreams started when I was very young, five or six. He always appeared to me at the same age I was. We sort of grew up together. He'd been a friend, confidante, and playmate. Lately the pull of attraction seemed to heighten each

29

time I dreamed of him. And because it was a dream, I could be everything that I wasn't in reality. Not that I knew how to do that.

I was lying under a weeping willow, mile long branches swept overhead. A babbling brook flowing over scattered bedrock sounded in the distance. The ambrosial smell of sweet pea tainted the air. A suitable surrounding for dreams made of fairy tales.

The sun was cast above. Gleaming rays speared through pockets in the willow tree. Lukas lay next to me on his side, fiddling with strands of grass. He eyed me coolly, waiting for me to turn towards him. In these dreams it seemed he waited for me. My brain was unexplainable.

"Brianna." His honey smooth voice spoke my name.

"Hi," I replied lamely. Even in my dreams I couldn't master being anything other than me.

He smiled at me brightly. His entire face beamed with a golden glow. "Long time, no see." He was lying beside me on the grass, propped up on the willow's trunk. Months had gone by since my last dream of him.

"I know. I was beginning to think you had forgotten about me."

He had one leg spread alongside me, and the other one bent up. "These are your dreams, remember?" he teased lightly.

He was always so carefree and happy, nothing seem to get to him. I had no idea how that felt. Responsibility seemed to be bred into my genes. We spent much of our time doing things I wouldn't dare do in my real life, and divulging parts of my life I was afraid to tell anyone else.

Today was no different.

"What's wrong?" he asked, his bright smile losing some of its shine.

Sitting up beside him on the trunk, I sighed. "What isn't wrong is the question."

He chuckled and brushed a stray hair from my eyes, tucking it behind my ear. His touch surged a blooming of warmth over me. "It can't be all that bad." Always the positive outlook for Lukas, his world was a cup half full.

Picking at the grass growing near the base of the willow, my problems came to the forefront of my mind. "In my case, it is," I grumbled, refusing to let go of my somber mood.

He looked amused by my discomfort. What is with all the guys being amused by me? I couldn't figure out why my thoughts continued to drift to Gavin. There was an extremely gorgeous guy in my dreams, and I was thinking about the rebel with the piercings. Maybe the problem was that Lukas wasn't real, and I wanted something real.

Even with the familiarity of Lukas, there had always

31

been an awareness of caution just under the surface. Although it never made much sense to me, so I ignored the warning. He was a dream after all. What harm can he possibly cause? Not to mention his attractiveness drew me. The more I dreamed of him, the closer I felt it. He was easy to be with. I should have just kissed him already. *It's not real*, I rationed. Better yet, I should have kissed Gavin when the chance presented itself, and a real possibility.

"Spill, we'll figure it out together." His encouragement was touching.

I looked out over the green valley. "I lost my temper today. It was bad," I revealed bleakly.

"Are you sure it was as bad as you think?" he asked knowing that I occasionally over exaggerate.

"I don't know. I guess if you consider grabbing a girls arm and leaving burn marks not bad then… yeah it wasn't bad," I snapped sarcastically.

His lips upturned at my melancholy disposition. "That's bad." He was trying to hide the smile that wanted to surface.

Playfully, I smacked him on the chest. "It was," I admitted. "She deserved it though," I defended, feeling the need to justify my actions.

"Of course she did. You wouldn't do anything that someone didn't deserve," he blithely teased.

Looking into his face I immediately thought about what a contrast he was to Gavin. Like the sun and the moon. Lukas was the boy next door with his wholesome good looks and lighthearted sense of humor. He had the kind of smile that you just had to answer in return. Gavin made me think of shadows, starlight nights and werewolves.

As soon as the thought fluttered through my head, the dream took a drastic change. My head was so filled with thoughts of Gavin and Lukas that it took moments for me to realize the shift.

Suddenly, the air surrounding us began to transform. The brightened sun was covered by the swift approach of dark, murky clouds. Threatening winds screamed and howled, whipping the branches in a war against us. It all happened so fast. I shuddered from the gloomy intensity.

Lukas grabbed my hand, pulling me sharply to my feet. "Hurry," he yelled over the deafening winds. Using himself as a shield from the slashing switch of tree limbs he guided us out from underneath – our feet crunching on fallen leaves. As we reached the edge of the covering, the willow's limbs transfigured into venomous snakes, the hissing of tongues seethed, and the clatter of tails echoed off the valley walls. At this point it was clear my subconscious was wacked.

An overpowering tug on my leg stopped me in my

33

tracks. Something held onto me squeezing in a deathly pressure. Glancing down, I found a snake coiled around my leg. A piercing scream ripped from my lungs, ringing over the valley. Lukas turned and expounded a hushed string of words over the chaotic noise.

I couldn't make out what he said over the racket and my own trepidation.

Just as abrupt, a ghostly silence erupted, followed by an eerie ambiance filling the valley. The wavering of my breath thundered in my ears over the muteness. He pulled me protectively to his side keeping his arm around me.

"Are you hurt?" He hastily looked me over to verify himself.

Before I had the option to answer, a smoldering ash of solid fog spread – engulfing us. Quickly I reached for his arm. I wasn't fast enough. My hands were filled with nothingness. Panic started to rise in my chest; my voice was filled with the prickling of hysteria as it pealed out.

"Lukas!" I yelled. "Lukas… where are you?" My voice came across pitchy. Tentatively I listened for his response; only to hear the quick fear of my short pants.

A dark husky voice broke into the wall of thickening air. "Bri!" it called.

A quivering of dread encumbered me as my head

whipped back and forth. Searching. Taking a step in retreat and another, I looked for an opening in the compacted haze. My eyes burned as I scanned for the image to the voice.

There was something familiar about the voice. It tugged at my mind. Then it clicked. If I had not just heard the voice earlier today, I wouldn't have been able to place it. As recognition seeped through, my pounding heart receded slowly.

"Gavin?" I whispered half to myself in confusion.

Turning in circles, the toe of my shoe bumped into a rock embedded in the ground, sending me sprawling. Landing with a groan, I barely caught my face from connecting with the surface. As I lay there stunned, a band of arms wrapped around me, pulling me carefully to my feet. Even without looking I knew it was Gavin. His scent was like a wild forest assaulting my insides.

I rubbed my hands over my now scraped and throbbing forearms. Fireflies spread through my stomach like wildfire at his proximity. Even in my dreams he caused those pesky fireflies.

"What are you doing here?" I asked dumbfounded. This was a dream, it didn't need logic, but his presence puzzled me. Never has there been anyone else in the dream except Lukas and me. His manifestation startled me, along with the creepy scenario. Nightmares weren't normally part of the deal. Today

35

was just full of bombshells.

His eyes alert, scanned beyond me. I wasn't sure how he was able to see past the smog. The attentive tension in his back caused a suspicion of unease to sprinkle along my spine.

"What is it?" I asked.

He never had a chance to answer my question, because that was the moment it ended.

I awoke with a sharp headache and lump lodged in my throat. Swallowing to stifle its pressure, I was shocked to find it scratchy, like I had been screaming. Pushing the bed covers aside I rolled off the bed and switched on the lamp, chasing the dark shadows from the walls. It was then I realized my body was trembling.

Facing the oval mirror on my dresser, I saw an unfamiliar reflection staring back. My skin was pale, covered with a sheen sweat, and my eyes were enlarged. The violet irises filled my glossy eyes. Running an unsteady hand through my hair, I forced myself to take deep even breaths.

"What the hell was that?" I voiced aloud, startled by the shakiness of my voice.

Leaving the light on, comforted by its soft glow, I crawled back into bed. Bracing my back against the headboard, I hugged my knees to my chest and forced the tense muscle to relax. My mind swirled around the dream, and the sense of reality that was still with me. I'd never had a dream with such clarity and devastating effects. Rarely was I prone to nightmares. Even as a child, however this exceeded anything I'd experienced or wish to again.

"Something is seriously wrong with me," I murmured. I must be getting sick. Lifting a hand to my forehead I expected a temperature, but I was sorely disappointed.

Eventually I tried to lie back down. I closed my eyes, hoping that sleep would take me. To my utter avail it proved impossible. Sleep was beyond my control, so I rendered the effort and laid there with the lamp shinning, waiting for the first signs of dawn.

As tired as I was in the morning, I forced my body to pay attention to my mind. *Must get up*, I chastised myself. Rubbing the sleep from my eyes I headed to the shower, cranking the heat with hope to chase the chills. Thank God it was Friday. The weekend was within reach, not that I had a life to boast about. My weekends were alternately spent at the shop.

The steam from the shower massaged my taunt nerves, as the memories of yesterday started flying in my head. This day couldn't end fast enough.

I donned my favorite outfit, a plum tank and my most flattering crystal-studded jeans, I needed comfort. And maybe the need to look good, would overrule the stress under my eyes.

Better to face your problems head on than to run and hide. I don't know who said that, but they definitely didn't have my problems.

CHAPTER 4

THE TOP WAS DOWN ON my very used black mustang, its engine roared like a big Herculean cat. To drown the noise and my nerves, I turned the radio a few octaves higher than comfort, One Republic's *Apologize* crooning from the speakers. The seats vibrated in time with the bass. Carelessly my hair was tied in a ponytail, letting the wind caress my cheeks. The skies dejected clouds hung overhead in a display of chaos.

Just like my mood.

The middle of October had an aura of fall creeping closer. More storms would threaten the oceans as hurricane season started to settle in. Focusing my attention back to the road, the mustang effortlessly hugged a gentle curve. My Roxy messenger bag was thrown in the back seat as I pulled into the parking lot of Holly Ridge High. This was my senior year, and something told me it might just be a year I wouldn't forget.

The schools structure reminded me of an odd shaped *S*, with its faded red bricks reflecting the wear and tear it weathered. There was a sweeping pink dogwood in front of the main office with wooden benches flanking either side. A large cougar mounted over the front of the building, with the schools motto stretched across the top in bold black letters.

Maneuvering my slightly rusting mustang into a parking space, the lot was packed with second hand vehicles like mine. Occasionally there was the glimmer of something flashy like the silver Infinite next to me, I deliberately avoided it. The last thing I needed was to dent the luxury car with my peeling black paint.

I grabbed my bag out of the backseat and headed toward the lockers. Arriving at the rundown row of metal compartments, I started shuffling my books for my first class. Pulling out my U.S. History book with subdued enthusiasm, I was acutely aware of the murmuring hum from the students around me. The hall sounded like the swirling buzz of mosquitoes after a humid rainfall. The hope that the event of yesterday was old news, and my classmates had found some other gossip to spread perished.

Resigned to whatever fate was in store, I numbly headed to homeroom.

My first two classes went as expected. Nothing life threatening, just more of the hushed whispers I vaguely noticed anymore. Or maybe I just didn't care.

In between the following class, I stopped at my locker to switch books. Flinging my chem. text into my bag, I heard the locker beside mine squeak. In no mood for company I slung my bag over my shoulder ready to make a quick exit. Laying my hand on the door of the locker with every intention of slamming it shut, I averted my gaze to avoid the body against the lockers. In that quick movement a scent of reckless woods washed over me.

Silently I groaned. *What is with this guy?*

Rolling my eyes I angled towards him, not expecting to see his sapphire eyes pinning mine. Was I supposed to breathe when he looked at me like this? My annoyance was momentarily forgotten.

He smirked, moving the hoop in his lip slightly. "Hey Bri." The shortened name sounded so intimate when it came from his mouth, indicating he knew me on a more personal level.

I knew that if I stayed another minute with him, I was going to make a complete fool of myself, utterly not trusting that I wouldn't say something idiotic. Then there was his smirk I couldn't figure out. Was he laughing at me? Was he amused by me or did he just have an annoying smirk that I found charming and maddening all at the same time?

Shutting the locker, I moved to evade him. He shifted his unlaced boots in front of my path obstructing my escape.

"What's your deal?" I asked, sharper than intended and ended up running a nervous hand through my hair. My

41

emotions around him reminded me of a pinball machine, bouncing from one side to another. Up. Down. Left. Right.

His smile only widened. "You're the only person I know." He had an arrogant confidence about him. In his stance, the way he was sure of himself. Of course I would find that endearing as well. "I figured you could help…me find my next class," he replied at my confused look and gestured to the bag on my shoulder.

I snorted. "You're actually going to class today?" My disbelief was real. I wasn't sure what to expect from him or if we'd even meet again. My school was the only high school in town and fairly large, there were plenty of kids I didn't know. Not only that, but I didn't have the best social skills.

He moved a little bit closer to me, shutting out more of the activity in the halls. "It seemed like the best way to see you again, unless you're planning to skip…" His voice had dropped but lost none of its huskiness.

Had he just said he wanted to see me again? My brain couldn't process the idea. Skirting over what my mind couldn't believe I asked the obvious question. Clearing my throat, "What class do you have next?"

"Umm…" He pulled out a crumpled slip of white paper from the back pocket of his jeans. It was impossible not to notice how good he looked in them. He was dressed pretty much the same as yesterday, dark clothing that looked impeccable on him. "What period is it?" he asked.

"Third," I replied, perplexed by his lack of interest. If he didn't know what period it was, what was he even doing here?

He unraveled his class schedule looking for third period. I couldn't help but notice how a stray lock fell over his eyes when he bent to read the slip. My fingers itched to brush it back from his face. "Looks like I have chemistry. Room C102." He read off the schedule, ignoring the midnight strand of hair.

"*Great*," I replied a tad sarcastic. Wasn't that just my luck? It also happened to be my next class.

He raised his studded eyebrow at me.

"It's my next class." I echoed my own thoughts. Turning to head towards the C hall, he followed in step beside me, not missing a beat.

"Chemistry… this should be interesting."

Glancing sideways, I narrowed my eyes. He held my gaze with the promise of a secret he was unwilling to divulge. There was no doubt he understood my irritation. The longer I stared at the blue of his iris, the faster my heart sped, and the fireflies zoomed in my stomach.

"You have such unusual eyes," he finally stated. The

43

husky dark texture of his voice lulled over me and seriousness shone in his eyes. A contrast to the teasing quality I'd gotten use to from him.

I was stunned at what sounded like another compliment, especially since I had been admiring his eyes. I could have said the same about his, if my tongue wasn't tied in knots. We had yet to break contact.

As fate would have it, he ended up saving me from yet another disaster. My focus was entirely on him, and in rationalizing the incident, it boiled down to really being his fault. Fortunately for me, he was more aware of our surroundings.

I all but walked into one of the pillars edging the entrance to C hall. He casually placed a hand at the small of my back and gracefully on his part, glided me around the pillar. The contact of his hand on my back broke the staring spell and incited an all new set of excitement. Tingling sensations like tiny shooting stars burst throughout me. The intensity of it brought me back inside my head, as I realized a second before I almost whacked the column. My feet miss-stepped, and I stumbled on the frayed carpet.

I knew I wasn't extremely graceful, but around him I was downright klutzy. Afraid to meet his eyes again I kept my head straight. "Thanks," I muttered under my breath, trying to hide my mortification.

"Is this going to be a habit? Me saving you?" There was a chuckle to his words.

I just rolled my eyes. Besides, relief huddled over me now that he was back in teasing form. His serious flattery wasn't something I could handle.

We walked into Mr. Burke's class side-by-side. The majority of the class was already seated, and all eyes were on us. Gavin left my side, walking up to where Mr. Burke sat at the front of the class. He handed Mr. Burke a pink slip as I made my way over to my table. He looked to me and winked. A murmur of chatter zigzagged down the rows of desks. It wasn't enough that I caused a spectacle yesterday, now I had some new mysterious gorgeous guy flirting with me. Sinking further into my chair, I scowled at him.

By the time lunch rolled around I was in the need of some serious girl time, Austin included. There hadn't been a spare moment to spill my guts. I knew that both of them were concerned about me and were primed to interrogate. Like what the hell was I thinking or was I crazy? I had turned my phone off last night, bent on shutting myself off from the world.

Winding through the cafeteria, the smell of milk cartons, fries and all things greasy swarm the room. I spotted Tori at our table with Austin.

"Hey," I greeted, throwing my bag over the back of my chair while taking my seat.

I had no more than sat down when the chair in front of me pulled out and was filled by none other than the dark and mysterious – Gavin.

My heart thumped at the sight of him. "What are you doing?" Having him suddenly appear every time I turned around was grating on my already frazzled emotions. There was no downtime to calm the effect he enticed.

At his arrival, Austin and Tori both froze mid-bite, to my dismay, and gawked. There hadn't been time to fill in the events of the current soap opera I was living. My plan to spill my guts at lunch was now nixed.

"Keeping you company," he responded, meeting my glare with a mischievous grin. He held my eyes longer than comfortable but I couldn't look away. Finally he turned to Austin and Tori. "Hey, I'm Gavin," he introduced, dazzling them with a smile. Austin still had his mouth agape, looking star-struck. Tori thankfully had the decency to smile in return, instead of looking like a goon.

"Sorry," I mumbled. Why did he make me forget myself? "Austin, Tori this is Gavin. We met umm–" I stumbled to find a reasonable explanation without sounding like a dork. "Yesterday in the parking lot," I managed. The admission caused a faint blush to crawl on my cheeks as I remembered our meeting, so much for not sounding like a dork.

Tori's inquisitive gaze burned at my side. I shifted fretfully in my seat. No doubt there would be a lot to answer for when the two of them got me alone. Gavin was not the kind of guy you forgot to tell your best friends about. Something told me that there was a good possibility that I would get hurt if I wasn't careful around him.

Gavin's husky voice broke me out of my thoughts. "It was sort of a hit and run." His twinkling eyes met mine, as an uneasy cough escaped my mouth. As bad as the joke was, it felt wicked sharing in something only the two of us understood. I found it impossible to be irritated with him. But it didn't last long.

The moment was ruined by none other than Rianne. She strolled by, trailing a finger on the table and angled at Gavin. "Hey hottie." She all but purred her words. "Sure you don't want to join me?" she invited, batting her fake lashes. If I had to guess, I would say that just about everything about her was fake. Her obvious flirtations made me want to gag. Lucky for her I hadn't eaten yet.

"I'm good here." He didn't even spare her more than a polite glance, which she couldn't possibly understand. Boys did not ignore her. Not that I blamed them, she did look like

47

Barbie's slutty twin. Her fire engine red skirt barely covered her ass, and the black top was low enough to be outlawed at Hooter's.

"You'll change your mind." Her utter confidence made me nauseated. I'm sure that she couldn't imagine what he saw in me and my friends. She was popular and probably thought she was doing him a social favor, a once in lifetime opportunity. She teased her honey blonde hair between her fingers. Rianne had been bullying kids at our school far too long.

Looking directly into my eyes he replied, "I doubt it."

A genuine smile broke out over my face and was mirrored in his. Next to me I could hear the low snickering of my friends. In an attempt to put me down, her sweet flirty tone turned down right sour and nasty. "You better watch yourself," she threatened me. Apparently being rejected didn't bring out her bright side.

I really didn't want her to destroy the mood we had going again, but I couldn't just let it go. "Suck it," I cheerfully snapped. Classy I know. The damage was done, best to just go for it. Never do anything half ass – my new outlook on life.

She flipped her hair over her shoulder and sauntered to her clique of followers. A glimpse of her black thong peeked over the top of her skirt as she swayed her hips with more oomph than necessary.

Gavin laughed low in his throat. "That was fun."

I had to fight the urge to roll my eyes. His idea of fun and mine didn't even come close.

"Is your life always this entertaining?" There was a hint of expectancy in his voice.

My friends sneered. Okay I was prone to weird things happening around me, and I did have what I would call an explosive anger issue, but that didn't mean my life was a freaking side show.

I glared their way. "Hardly," I muttered.

By the time lunch ended, I'd picked my way through what food I had. My appetite was on the fritz. Tossing the remaining in the trash, I glared at Gavin and took off after my friends.

Walking side-by-side, both Austin and Tori's interest was piqued beyond control, now that we were alone. They stared at me gleaming, waiting for me to dish.

I rolled my eyes. "It was nothing. I ran into him when I left yesterday. Literally. End of story."

"Wait… he ditched yesterday also?" Tori asked, putting together the facts.

"I guess." I was reluctant to admit.

"He oozes trouble," Austin commented like it was hot.

"You're telling me," I grumbled under my breath.

"You better not let *that* slip away babygirl," he hollered as we split off to our separate classes.

The final bell sounded, piping into the classrooms during my French lesson and interrupting my traveling thoughts. Shuffling into the halls I weaved my way between the cluster of eager kids ready to kick start their weekend.

He was leaning casually up against the wall by my locker, one leg over the other. His stance was lazy and relaxed. Shifting my gaze to his face it skimmed the sharp angles that defined his jaw line. His black hair was edgy with stands that framed his searing sapphire eyes. Those eyes were thickly fanned by dark eyelashes. Gazing into the pools of blue, I realized that he was staring at me. His mouth upturned in a smirk. Mesmerized I watched as he played with the ring glittering his lower lip.

"So you made it through the whole day." His lips split into a knee-shattering smile.

I stared hard after him as he walked away and I was left with a bewildered expression on my face.

"Damn," I murmured, silently praying I wouldn't behave like a blubbering idiot the entire school year.

Dazed, I grumbled my way to the parking lot.

CHAPTER 5

EVERY OTHER SATURDAY I WENT into the shop at noon and usually stayed until closing. With Halloween around the corner, the displays and floral coolers were abundantly filled with the vibrant colors of fall, burnt oranges, deep reds and golden yellows. Tiger Lilies, marigolds, chrysanthemums and pansies showcased the majority of the collections.

There were the traditional spooky arrangements in shades of black and orange, sprinkled with glitter or ghostly accent pieces. The shop also stocked specialty items. Scattered between the floral designs were mystical figures, seasonal decorations, and artwork from local artists hung on the walls.

Homecoming just so happened to be this weekend. The orders for corsages and boutonnieres over the week had piled up and were now ready for pickup. With everything going on the last few days, the school event never even crossed my mind. I somehow in my distraction missed all the décor and posters that usually littered the school. Not that it made a difference.

Homecoming, or any other school function for that matter, really wasn't my thing. It was no surprise that I was relieved to be working.

The commotion of the event made the day fly by. Especially the last few hours before the dance began. Normally I just manned the counter, helped with customers and rung up sales. There were also two other part-time employees besides myself who helped out. Today it was just the two of us, and I had about reached my limit of baby's breath, roses, and dyed carnations. I was clueless to why my peers matched the flowers to the exact shade of their shoes or dress. Sadly, very few actually knew my name or that we attended the same school.

Missy Walters was one of the last to come in. Her sun-bleached hair was curly and cascading prettily over her exposed shoulders.

"Are you here to pick up a corsage?" I sweetened my voice like I hadn't uttered that phrase a hundred times before.

She nodded, sending her bouncing curls for a wild ride. "For Walters," she added, unaware that I already had her corsage in hand. She wasn't the brightest crayon in the box.

"Do I know you?" Her voice was fit for a little girl, all cutesy.

"Umm… yeah, I think we have Interior Design together, fifth period" I replied offhandedly, while tying a ribbon on the box of her corsage.

She popped her pink gum and giggled. "Oh yep, that's it. You sit in the back row."

Actually I sat in the second row, but for her it was close enough. I don't how she heard herself over all the snapping of the gum, so I just nodded in agreement.

"Well thanks for the flowers." She smiled when I passed her the package.

"Have fun tonight," I called as she headed for the exit. I wanted to make sure she heard me over the gum smacking.

"Sure thing, you too." Her voice was over bubbly, like her gum.

Oh loads I thought mockingly. I had big plans for tonight that involved the snugness of my bed, and the current Nora Roberts book I was reading.

The chime on the door rang near the end of the night while I was wiping down the counter. We had an hour left before the shop closed, but most everything had been cleaned, straightened and restocked. I stopped what I was doing to greet the customer, absently tucking a hair behind my ear.

"Hi, is there something –" The rest fell from my lips. Tingles danced down my back, and then I realized who came through the door.

Gavin, in his dark jeans, strolled across the room to where I stood behind the glass counter. The clatter of his half untied boots echoed at his approach.

"Actually there is something you can help me with." He

reached the counter and stood in front of me, leaning a hip against the glass.

I ignored his words. "Are you stalking me?" I was stunned by that fact that he was standing in front of me.

"That's not exactly the greeting I was hoping for." He leaned in, smiling at me with teasing eyes.

"So you are stalking me?" I smiled back. No idea where that came from. I hadn't the first clue how to flirt.

"No actually…"

And that was all I needed for my mind to go off on a tangent. What if he'd actually come in to buy something? I assumed he was here for me, but what if he wasn't. Maybe he was here to pick-up flowers for homecoming. It was late – but not enough so that he couldn't still go to the dance. My heart sunk at the image of him dancing with another girl. He might be new here, but he would have no trouble finding a date. Hell it was possible that Rianne had asked him. She made her interest overtly clear at lunch. How soon my mind had forgotten that he had shut her down.

He watched me as my mind ran through the entire horrible scenario before finishing. "I wanted to ask you something."

I swallowed back the large lump that suddenly formed in my throat. "Sorry, long day." I pasted on a smile, yielding.

Internally, I scolded myself to be as polite as I could be. "Are you picking up an order?" I assumed, trying to keep my voice even and the disappointment from it.

He played with the hoop on his bottom lip – absently twirling it. "No." His brows drew together at my assumption. "But I was hoping you were almost done here?" There was a touch of hesitancy to his voice, completely out of character for his normally cocky attitude.

Wide-eyed and tongue-tied I went all spacey. He really had to stop doing that to me.

"I was hoping you could show me what people did for fun around here," he continued after I failed to have a coherent thought. I never even heard my aunt return from the backroom in the middle of his invitation.

She smiled brightly over his shoulder at me as she made her way around the counter. Gavin straightened slightly at her approach. His gaze went from mine to hers.

"Hi, I'm Clara – Brianna's aunt." She grinned at him sincerely. "Are you a friend of hers?" She was fishing for information, more specifically if he was something more than a *friend*. I couldn't blame her inquisition. A hot guy in the shop asking me on what could be misconstrued for a date was a rare commodity. Or in my case…unheard of.

Not giving him the opportunity to give her false hope I

quickly recovered and cut in. My aunt didn't have a judgmental bone in her body. Everyone got an equal chance until you deserved otherwise. But I think her genuine acceptance caught Gavin a little off guard. Well I assumed that was why he looked at her cautiously, like she might toss him out at any moment.

"He just moved here," I lamely answered with more volume than I meant to. I took a quick breath. "We met a few days ago at school." This time I lowered my tone but raced my words. The whole situation was making me jumpy.

"Hmm…" My aunt pursed her slightly grinning lips, no doubt picking up my odd behavior.

This was not going at all like I would have hoped. Not that I had even a second to think about what was happening here.

"I was just asking Bri if she would like to show me around town. That is, if you don't mind?"

She raised her eyes at the nickname, and I could see her internal mind making all kinds of wrong assumptions. "*Bri* would love to." She excitedly agreed on my behalf.

"I could drop her off at home afterwards. I'll make sure it's not too late," he added.

"Perfect, she'll be ready in a few." She took my place behind the counter, gently nudging me into action.

What?

I will?

I don't know how everything had spun out of my control. They were talking as if I wasn't there or didn't have a say in the matter. Maybe I didn't want to go. Totally not true but at the least I should be the one to say yes or no. I mean the idea of spending an entire evening with Gavin was both elating and frightening. The fireflies danced in my belly.

"I haven't finished –" My aunt interrupted my protest. I wasn't against going out with Gavin; I don't know anyone who would be. I was just slightly infuriated about being sneakily maneuvered.

"Don't worry. I got it covered. Go. Have fun," she rebuked.

I eyed her, letting her know I wasn't happy about being finessed. "I'll be ready in a minute," I mumbled.

Surrendering my fate, I headed to the backroom. I did what I could with what I had. Quickly I ran a brush through my hair, reapplied my eyeliner and mascara, and coated on my favorite strawberry flavored lip gloss. Luckily we don't have any kind of uniform at the shop. Usually I just wore whatever. Today it was a black halter and jeans. At least they made my butt look good. *Thank goodness for small wonders*. Digging through my bag, I pulled out a pair of silver dangling earrings and fitted them in the holes.

This was the best I could do under the circumstances.

Walking back into the shop, he was casually conversing with my aunt. They both looked to me at my approach.

"Ready." He lifted the brow with the sterling bar in it.

I just nodded my head and waved good-bye to my aunt. She mouthed *have fun* and grinned from ear-to-ear.

He led me to a sleek and shiny car that probably cost more than my aunt's and mine combined. Coming around to the passenger side, he opened my door. The gesture was completely sweet, unexpected, and made me extremely self-conscious.

"Thanks," I muttered.

He drove an old school black '69 Charger. At least that's what he told me. It looked like it was straight out of the showroom. Not exactly the car that came to mind for him. I envisioned him on a motorcycle, something more daring. But once the engine howled to life, thundering with the powerful rumble, I got the appeal. Strapping on my seatbelt, I buckled in for what proved to be a very fast ride.

The radio was on low, pumping an alternative band. His interior was clean. It smelled of leather and exotic woods. If someone had told me last week that I would be going out on a Saturday night with an extremely drool-worthy guy, I would have asked them what kind of crack they were smoking. Honestly, I figured I wouldn't date until I got to college. There would be a fresh batch of hotties who wouldn't know me, a whole world of opportunities.

Look at me now. I was on my first *almost* real date. Hold the presses.

"Where to?" He looked over at me for direction.

He was so asking the wrong person. "There really isn't anything fun to do here," I reluctantly admitted. I didn't want him to know how boring my life really was.

"Well in that case, I guess we'll have to make our own fun." He smiled devilishly at me from across the seat. "What's open late?"

That grin was going to get me in trouble. I was sure.

We ended up at a little coffee shop near the edge of town that I went to often. Carmel Macchiato had become a self-indulging addiction I took every advantage of. Taking a seat in a quiet section near the back, we sat opposite of each other. The place had a scattered array of patrons sipping on steaming mugs, tapping away on laptops, or sucking on frozen concoctions gossiping.

There were multi-colored hanging lights casting a low glow, giving a secluded atmosphere. Each table had three tealight candles flickering in unruliness.

Immediately upon sitting we were greeted by a young girl, Carla her nametag claimed. She couldn't have been much older than me, and her eyes were glued on Gavin. Invisibility wasn't a foreign feeling. Her uniform was a little tight, and I was afraid she was going to fall out of the top.

Folding my hands on the table, I watched her soak up the sight of him. Steeling a glance, I noticed a strange spark about his eyes. They were normally pools of deep blue, but this was something else. Blinking to clear the glare of the soft light above, he turned and asked what I would like. Whatever I thought I saw, was gone.

"Carmel macchiato," I said on auto-response, still wondering what just happened.

Smiling, he gave Carla my order and his, coffee black. Carla scurried to get our drinks. I don't remember the service being this good. The coffee is great, but the service was usually crap.

"So is it just you and your aunt?" He casually inquired bringing my focus back to the present.

"Yeah, my parents died when I was five," I confessed and glanced around the room. My paranoia must be setting in, it was either that or everyone was staring at us.

"That must have been hard." There was sincerity and compassion in his expression.

I shrugged. "I don't really remember it much. It's always been the two of us." I kept taking a peek to see if anyone was looking our way.

"And what about your other relatives? Do you see them?" He was just full of questions.

I hadn't thought about my family in some time. My aunt was mostly it. I did have a grandma on my mom's side that I visited, but I couldn't picture one face from my dad's side. "I have a grandma not far from here, but no one else really," I admitted, slightly sadden by the lack of people in my life. "What about you?" It was time to turn the table. "Do you have any siblings?"

He relaxed his posture and smirked. That said everything. He adored his family. "I have an older brother and a younger sister. Jared is in college and Sophie is a sophomore."

"At our school?" I was taken by surprise that I hadn't seen her yet.

He nodded his dark head. "I'm sure you'll see her around. She is eager to meet you."

"You told her about me?" My tone skeptical.

He laughed. The huskiness of it flooded over me and packed my belly with the heat of fireflies. "It's kind of unavoidable. She has a way of pulling information out of you without you knowing. A small talent of hers, you'll see what I mean."

Carla returned with our drinks and asked Gavin pointedly if there was anything she could do for him. I fought the urge to kick her from under the table, anything to get her attention elsewhere.

"That will be all thanks," he graciously dismissed her.

"Is your sister psychic or something?" I teased.

He grinned. "Not quite."

"Okay now I'm intrigued and a little afraid." I took a sip of my macchiato and closed my eyes as the sweet flavor hit my tongue. Swallowing the hot liquid I opened my eyes to find Gavin staring intently at me. They lured me into unexplored territory.

"You are not at all like I thought." There was a low husky strain to his voice.

His admission caused a powerful flush that had nothing to do with the coffee and everything with the way he looked at me. Absently turning the cup in my hand I tentatively asked, "I'm not?"

He stared, looking at me like I was a mystery waiting to be solved, totally ironic considering I was trying to do the same with him. Apparently neither of us could figure the other out.

"No, you have my mind spinning in circles. I can't

figure you out," he admitted not entirely happy about it.

"What's there to figure out? I'm just a girl from a small town."

Turning away he sighed. "I don't know. It's more complicated." He tugged on his lip ring looking lost in thought. "Come on… I should get you home," he said before I could ask him what was so complicated. I wanted to press the subject, but the confusion in his expression stopped me.

The car ride to my house was death-defying. He drove at speeds I had never ventured to. Yet somehow I never felt like my safety was threatened. Everything about this guy screamed danger, but I didn't believe it.

The porch light shined as he walked to me to the front door. I shuffled my feet on the sandy wood planks. That was one of the downfalls of living by the ocean, there was sand everywhere.

He held out his hand. "Let me see your phone."

I eyed him wearily, but gave it over. Our fingers touched for a split moment, and a static shock like static tingled at the spot where our fingers met.

If he had felt anything, he never led on. Scrolling through the menu, he punched on the keys. There wasn't much light on the porch so I couldn't see what he was doing.

"There." He handed the device back.

"Thanks, I think." I stood in front of him, shuffling my feet uncertain how to say goodbye. When he traced his fingertips alongside my face, tucking loose strands behind my ear, a bolt of shock and something more caused my head to snap up.

His eyes glimmered, but I swear behind the twinkle was a hint of regret. "Sweet dreams Bri."

Walking inside the house, I leaned up against the closed door. The roar of his engine rippled through the night, and I sighed with a content smile on my lips.

CHAPTER 6

THE NEXT MORNING I WOKE up mystified. On one hand I was ecstatic about spending time with Gavin. On the other he was a puzzle. I was pretty good at puzzles so the idea of trying to figure him out was appealing to my nature. As I lay there staring at the ceiling, I tried to sort out the little I already knew about him. I couldn't let go of this nudge that there was something peculiar about him. Call it a hunch or whatever, but it gnawed at the back of my mind.

Sunday's were lazy. I didn't work and mostly spent the day catching up on household chores, finishing my homework, and watching my DVR. Regrettably I got up when it became clear I wasn't going to get any answers glaring at the ceiling. Pulling a hoodie over the tank I slept in, I padded my way downstairs.

My aunt was at the breakfast bar with her morning coffee, the aroma tempting. "Morning," she beamed between sips of her steaming mug.

There was a hint of something sweetening the air mixed with the bitter coffee grounds. Plopping down on a burgundy stool, I ran a hand through my tousled hair and grumbled an incomprehensible response.

"Coffee?" She spun around going to the pot still on the warmer.

Our kitchen was ornamented in cranberries and ivy. They were woven around the chains of the chandelier and intricately staggered above the dark cherry cabinets. The whole ensemble had a country living vibe.

Nodding my head, she set a roasting cup in front of me. Placing my hands on either side of the mug, I let the warmth soak into them.

"I made cinnamon rolls if you would like one," she offered, leaning her elbows on the counter grinning at me.

It was killing her, waiting for me to say something about last night. She was all but bursting with fervent impatience. I glanced over at the clock and noticed there were only a few more minutes before she needed to leave for the shop.

"You're killing me." She echoed my thoughts.

I rolled my eyes. "It was nothing," I insisted.

She didn't believe me. "He sure didn't look like nothing."

You're telling me. "I know… this is so bad," I whined, shoving my face into my hands.

She laughed at my theatrics. The sound was like home. Comfort. Security.

"I think he wants to be *friends*," I scoffed. The last word was said with annoyance.

"The way that boy looked at you was anything but *just friends*. Give it time, you'll see. For now be yourself. He won't be able to resist."

Who was she kidding? How was I supposed to be myself when I rarely even knew who that was?

Exhaling I said, "I think I'll take one of those cinnamon rolls now."

Placing the sticky bun on a plate she handed it to me. "I can't believe my angel has a boyfriend." She had a silly grin on her face.

Groaning, I laid my head on the countertop. "He is not my boyfriend." The words were muffled by the granite.

"See you by five," she called over her shoulder and headed to the garage.

***

The DVR was currently playing the previous week's episode of my favorite series. I had my feet tucked beneath me; a blanket wrapped around my legs, and I still wore the hoodie from this morning. The bad reality show on the screen only had part of my attention. Before I could prevent it, the memory of last night with the sinister Gavin came back to taunt me. What was it about him that caused my hairs to stand up and get my blood pumping all at the same time?

He struck a chord in me, and I started to regret not pressing him on our *complication*. Maybe that was part of his angle, to remain aloof and mysterious to keep me interested. Little did he know, I was way past just interested. I might have just slammed into what I was sure was an unhealthy obsession. Why couldn't I get him out of my head?

Halfway into the show, my phone vibrated on the cushion beside me. Unlocking the home screen the text icon blinked with a new message.

What are you doing? It read, popping up Gavin's name next to the message. The secret of my phone last night revealed itself. He must have added himself to my contacts.

Nothin. Did you steal my number also? I sent the response with a squiggling smiley face.

The phone hummed again seconds later. **One of my many tricks.**

Oh I'm sure it is. Grinning I tapped away on the keys. **I would have given it to you.**

Not as much fun!

And you're all about fun... I replied.

There's nothing wrong with a little fun. You going to school tomorrow?

I rolled my eyes after reading the last text. **Where else**

would I be?

Somewhere with me?

Funny… See you in Chem.

Ugh… Fine. If that's the only way I can see you. I could almost hear the aggravation in his text.

Returning my attention to the last half of my show, the night wore on. And on. And on.

Finally, out of sheer boredom I climbed the stairs to the sanctuary of my room. My homework was done and the laundry washed.

God, I was so lame.

The walls glistened in lilac frost accentuated by the silvery moss comforter that lain spread across my bed. There were always fresh flowers in the vase at my nightstand, a perk for having an aunt who owned a floral shop. I believed the current flower was hydrangea filling my room with its sugary aroma.

I whipped my hoodie off in the corner and headed to the small desk housing my ancient, barely functioning laptop. Hitting the power switch I waited for it to boot up. My mind wandered against my will. His dark poetic features clearly impressed into my memory.

Heaving a deep sigh, I shook my head mentally trying to erase his hotness.

The homepage on my computer loaded, and I logged in to checking my emails. Nothing significant, a bunch of spam, a few jokes from Austin, and one from school reminding me to sign up for email updates on my grades. I sifted through the junk, read Austin's and sent most to my trash folder. Frustrated with the snail speed of my internet connection I shut the computer down and closed it with a satisfying snap.

This day dragged butt.

Grabbing my iPod, I flung myself on the bed and scrolled down the long menu of songs. I selected a loud angry Alanis Morissette track and pumped up the volume. I was determined to drown out all images of Gavin Mason, steaming ones included.

The dream hit me faster than ever. One instant I was listening to Alanis belt '*You, you, you oughta know*'. And the next I was in a clearing, enclosed by fields of lavender. The transition was typically gradual. When I closed my eyes there was usually some interlude to let my body and mind unwind. This time it was like being sucked down a water slide.

Lukas was sitting next to me, close enough that I felt the brush of his arm. It was easy comfort with him. The sandy blonde of his hair moved slightly with the gentle breeze that mixed with the lavender essence. His emerald eyes sought mine.

"Hey." The warmth of his breath flushed my cheeks.

"Hi," I replied. "I didn't think I'd see you so soon."

He smiled charmingly, illuminating the golden boy face. "Me either…I'm not complaining though."

At times he seemed too good to be true or in this case dream about. I was pretty sure my mind wasn't that ingenious.

"Earth to Brianna," he called mockingly.

"What?" I startled from the random thoughts.

He was eyeing me coolly. "You were a million miles away."

I huffed. "Sorry, it's been a hectic week," I apologized.

Taking both my hands in his, he pulled me effortlessly to my feet. "Good, let's do something." The head rush caused a little hitch in my breathing. "Come on," he said a second before taking off into the meadow of lavender, his golden hair bouncing with his hurried movements.

Not missing a beat, I bolted out after him. "Lukas!" I shouted. "You better not lose me." Forgetting that he was way more athletically built than most guys at my school, he could have been a track star. Yet this was a dream, so how far could he really go?

Well it seemed pretty far because it wasn't long before I lost sight of him, or he was in an extremely great hiding spot.

Reaching the edge of a pond immersed with lily pads, I

paused in my search. My lungs were ragged from chasing and then losing him. Maybe it was time I hit the gym. Before I caught my breath, he snuck up behind me. Encircling his arms around my waist, he spun me in dizzying circles. His arms felt amazing. Real or not I still appreciated being held by him. I collapsed us to the ground. He took full advantage of his position and tickled me until I couldn't breathe. I choked on my laughter.

"Stop," I sobbed between giggling gasps.

His fingers hitting just the right spots to make me curl in tickled torture. "What did you say, more? It's hard to understand you when you're laughing so hard," he teased in his honey smooth voice.

"For real – can't – breathe," I spit out between gasps. Playfully I knocked at his hands.

"Okay, okay… I give," he conceded, but grinned impishly. He rocked back into a sitting position, swiping grass off his clothes.

Smiling into his emerald eyes I felt a huge boulder lifted from my back. A few stolen moments of childish pleasure relaxed my body. I felt weightless.

"You have no idea how special you are." His dreamy voice had softened.

Who doesn't dream of a guy saying those exact words?

The problem was… it was a dream. I fleetingly pictured Gavin's dark looks, and his smirk that was becoming all too sexy.

"I'm really not," I protested. "I'm just some girl."

"Not just any girl – trust me."

Trust him. Did I, trust him? How could some mysterious guy show up in my life and I trusted him uncomplicatedly, but I couldn't decide if I did indeed trust Lukas, who I've dreamed of for forever.

Our feet dangled over the ponds edge. He sighed, the carelessness gone. "Who was the guy that showed up last time?" There was a disapproving edge to his tone. He tried to hide it.

Strange that for only a moment Gavin had been on my mind and now Lukas was asking about him. Anxiously I shrugged. "No one."

He arched an eye.

"Okay, he's a new guy at school," I confessed.

His lips thinned in a straight line. "Is he something more?" There was a detested quality about the way he asked, like a bad after taste.

"No," I said shaking my head. "Just a friend. Why?" I wanted to know why he even cared.

"It was just… weird."

I assumed he was referring to the nightmare ending from our previous encounter. Weird was an understatement. I was still unclear how my mind came up with these dreams. "It was weird. I don't understand any of this." I threw my hands in the air on a whim of aggravation.

"Were you thinking of him while you were with me?" he asked, a speck of jealousy lacing it.

I didn't like the insinuation behind his tone, like I'd done something wrong. Chewing at the bottom of my lip, I contemplated my answer. No matter that Lukas was being unreasonable I didn't want to hurt him. Was it possible to hurt a dream's feelings, because that's what I was afraid would happen.

Craziness.

"I don't know…I guess I was," I grudgingly admitted. "Does it make a difference whether I was or not?"

The expression in his face fell, and it sunk my heart. "Not really. I'm just not used to sharing you. You've never brought anyone else into the dreams."

True I hadn't, but I never really realized that I could. I mean it hadn't been intentional. I thought about Gavin, and somewhere my subconscious had thought it was a good idea to include him to the mix. Regardless that it ended in a very hot mess. My mind was playing tricks with me.

I'm sorry," I said sincerely. "I'll try not to do it again."
Was I really apologizing for something I couldn't control? I
wanted to appease him, to see the lightness in his emerald eyes.
Not the heavy emotion that shone. It didn't feel right upsetting
Lukas, I mean what harm could it do appeasing my
imagination. He seemed satisfied with my admission – for
now.

Entwining our fingers, he played with our hands. "I
believe you."

Well that only made one of us, because I wasn't so sure
I could stop thinking about Gavin any more than I could stop
dreaming about Lukas. Just his name was enough to have my
heart race, even while I was sleeping. As guilty as it made me
feel when I was dreaming of Lukas, I couldn't stop my mind
from drifting to Gavin. Lukas used to be all I dreamed of. I
don't know what changed, which made it worse because he
was also aware of the alteration. The whole situation bothered
me more than it should. Especially considering none of it was
real.

As if on cue from my straying thoughts of Gavin, a
growling roar erupted.

I awoke with the sound still ringing in my ears.

CHAPTER 7

THE FOLLOWING WEEKS AT SCHOOL were the most exciting. Gavin made my day. His mysterious presence in my daily life was becoming something I depended on. My friends casually accepted the newcomer as part of our group as easily as he'd fit into mine. Austin found him extremely sexy, like a magazine cover he could ogle and appreciate. Tori was more watchful. She was aware that there was something between us but couldn't figure it out. There was no denying the attraction we sparked, yet both of us tried to tramp it.

And Rianne, well she continued to eye me with disdain.

There was a connection between Gavin and I that I couldn't ignore. However, I was no closer to figuring out his angle. And meeting his sister only amplified my inkling that something was different about them, and it had nothing to do with his dark and dangerous looks. I couldn't pinpoint what it was. Something inside me demanded that there was more to him than he let on.

I met his sister in the parking lot Wednesday morning on my way into school. She had ridden with Gavin. I caught my first glimpse of her as I stepped out of my car. He pulled in beside me. Each morning the rumble of his engine announced his arrival and sent my innards on a roller coaster. I wouldn't be surprised if I started getting ulcers from the amount of activity my stomach went through around him. It couldn't possibly be healthy for me.

Stepping from the passenger side, she wasn't at all what I expected. I pictured a hardass with purple hair, raccoon makeup and Goth wear. What I got was an eyeful of an intimidating beauty. She had the shiniest midnight hair that blanketed her shoulders and framed her delicate face. Her eyes were the same piercing blue as Gavin's but outlined with thick lush lashes. The floor length dress she wore had a hippy vibe and contoured to her perfect body in a way that I envied. She was downright stunning and immediately inviting.

"You must be Brianna." Her voice sung in the morning air like a hummingbird. "I've heard so much about you," she admitted before Gavin jabbed her playfully in the side. "What?" She batted her lashes innocently. "You're all he's talked about since we moved here," she softly added as we walked toward the lockers.

"Sophie," he growled low in warning.

She was unfazed by him. "I'm Sophie." She smiled with genuine warmth.

"Wow, you are really pretty," I lamely complimented and cringed inside. Sometimes things shot out of my mouth that I could thump myself over the head for. This was one of those times.

She tossed her head over her shoulder at Gavin. "I like her already." He trailed behind us. Glancing back at me she enclosed me in her liveliness. Sophie was such a disparity to Gavin's dark and brooding looks. I wouldn't have guessed them brother and sister if it weren't for the eyes. "I don't know how you stand this brutes company." Her musical tone lit with bantering affection.

"It's a gift. I'm irresistible," Gavin stated smirking.

We both snorted and then smiled at each other over our duel action.

"Please, don't flatter yourself," she countered. Their sibling repartee was amusing and reminded me how much I missed out on not having a brother or sister.

Her hand causally looped my arm with hers, spurring a zing comparable to the one I occasionally felt with Gavin. Yet not exactly, with her it didn't have the essential tension. It lacked the zeal of intensity. Everything with Gavin was intense. Her familiar eyes quickly sought mine, judging my reaction. I knew then that the energy, or whatever it was, meant something. Recovering quickly, I didn't want to let on that I thought something was amiss. We walked side-by-side into the school.

"I don't know many people yet, and I know you're a senior, but… maybe we could hang out sometime? My family would love to meet you."

"Sure, I would like that." And I was being sincere. I initially thought her beauty would intimidate me, but just as quickly I realized there was kinship I rarely felt, something in her hummingbird voice that I had an affinity with.

Her smile twinkled in excitement. "See you later." She gave me a quick hug. Sophie was impossible not to like. I sucked with people, but I felt like I had just made an ally and hopefully a friend.

"I'm going to kill her," he half-heartedly threatened when Sophie was out of reach.

Walking next to me, his arm brushed mine occasionally. "Why?" I wondered aloud. He smelled like heaven.

"Why? Because that was embarrassing," he confessed, grinning sheepishly.

I laughed at his uneasiness. "Hardly…she's amazing."

"Amazingly annoying."

"She's your sister. What does that make you?"

He smirked recovering his insolence. "Dashing."

So true. I rolled my eyes as he opened the door to my first class. "See you in Chem."

"Wouldn't miss it," he assured, and then strolled across the hall to his class.

Chemistry soon became my favorite class, and it had nothing to do with atoms, molecules or particles. I always thought of myself as an English buff, how quickly that can change. Gavin somehow had found a way to finagle his way into becoming my lab partner. I haven't the slightest idea how. Before he joined the class my partner had been Adam Joyhart. The class had been equally divided, with Gavin's addition he should have been just added to a group. Instead Mr. Burke moved Adam to another pair and assigned Gavin as my partner. I was tempted enough to ask Gavin about it, but he just shrugged it off.

We walked into class together and took a seat at our table. He made a habit of showing up at my locker each day and walking me to class – a gentleman behind the badass.

Mr. Burke immediately started in on his lesson about Conversion of Mass. I glanced down at my notes for the last week. They were practically non-existent. I had found that with Gavin beside me, my note taking abilities sucked. He clogged my brain cells. Even with the extra studying at my house, I'd be lucky to pass this class. A hard concept for an almost straight A student.

"You want to hang out tonight?" he whispered, leaning

in close to my ear. His breath tickled the back of my neck, causing the tiny hairs to spike. If I turned my head a fraction in his direction, it would be incredibly simple to press our lips together. Failing this class was proving to be worth the risk.

Focusing my thoughts on inhaling and exhaling and not on his pleasurable proximity, I softly replied, "Sure."

At this point I am completely tuned out of the lecture, my dilemma clear. Mr. Burke shoving his glasses back up the bridge of his nose and rambled on in monotones about isolated systems. No idea.

"Better bring your notes," he smirked, gesturing to the blank page in front of me.

Groaning, I laid my head on my arms. How had he woven his way so intently in my life?

Chemistry always ended too soon, and it had absolutely nothing to do with the topic. The remaining of my classes was a drag compared to third period. I should be thankful he was only in one of my classes. I couldn't imagine how my grades would suffer.

During the middle of my ninth period French lesson, I started to daydream. I don't know why Lukas came to mind, yet as in most of my thoughts of Lukas, I couldn't help smiling and imagining his boyish, charming looks. The sunny warmth I always found with him, not like the eruptive feelings Gavin

81

gave me. Lukas was calm, steady and spirited. Everything I wasn't.

Our conversation the other night started playing through my head. The way things ended, tugged at my heart as I remembered the hurt and disappointment swimming in his eyes. I never in my wildest dreams (no pun intended) thought that my day life would compete with my night life so to speak. The fact that Lukas knew about Gavin, but Gavin didn't know about Lukas, well in some bizarre and misplaced way it made me feel dishonest and regretful. Like I was cheating on one of them, which was completely insane since in reality I wasn't dating either one of them. Not that I wouldn't if I was given the opportunity. Maybe that was it. Maybe somewhere deep inside me I was holding out for one of them. Again how any of this made sense was beyond my comprehension. It was inhumanly possible for me to even have a *normal* relationship with Lukas. Why did I continue to torment myself with possibilities that weren't there?

My impractical internal struggle was interrupted by the familiar buzzing of my phone. I carefully snuck it from the front pocket of my jeans. We weren't allowed to text during class, but that hardly stopped anyone. The trick was to not get caught.

Tori's name blinked under new messages. **Mall on**

Friday? It was followed by a line of smileys.

We hadn't hung out in a millennium. My life lately was divided between Gavin and the shop. He'd come over on the nights I didn't work in the disguise of doing our chemistry assignments, which of course we did – or I did. There were always a few tense moments that boiled my blood. Our friendship or whatever we had going progressed rapidly. I didn't want Tori to feel ignored. And the blame weighed heavily on my decision.

I inconspicuously texted back as my French teacher lectured on our vocabulary.

Sure... I'll pick you up after school.

Great I'm in need of some therapy.

I grinned at my phone. Only Tori could think of spending her dad's money as therapy.

CHAPTER 8

THE MALL ON A FRIDAY night wasn't exactly my venue of choice. I enjoyed shopping like the majority of girls; I just like to do it without the crowds. Tori was a shop-a-holic. While I spent most of my time window shopping, she needed a valet to help her to the car. My part-time check only went so far. But when you had a credit card with daddy's infinite limit on it, I might enjoy the experience at a whole new level.

For someone who never had to worry about money, Tori was the least snobbish person I knew. She shopped – I read. Somewhere along the lines of first grade we became friends and found a balance between the two.

High-end shops lined the shopping center on two floors, the ones were they pumped perfume or cologne throughout the store so when you walked by it tempted you with a fragrance of seduction. Located at the heart of the mall was the food court. Tonight the over-priced stores were jammed with teenagers causing a ruckus. Guys scoping out desperate girls with too much make-up, wearing clothes two-sizes too small. Rianne totally came to mind. I gave up on the whole mall scene while Tori found it mildly amusing. The lack of entertainment was evident in my peer's choice of hangouts.

"Check out the buns on Mr. Abercrombie," she said to a guy we passed on the escalator.

I elbowed her in the side. "Focus."

"Oh I get it. Now that you have a hot guy to drool over the rest of us have suffer without. At least let me check out the merchandise."

I laughed. She could be so dramatic when she wanted to be. I always felt so responsible when we were together. She had such a careless air about her. "You can look, but no touching."

"What fun is that? Austin wouldn't mind." There was amusement in her voice.

She could get me in so much trouble. *Trouble* should have been her middle name.

"Fine," I said. "Let's look."

"That's more like it," she purred and had me laughing.

"Check out blondie over by Aeropostale. I bet you could eat off his abs." There was practically drool foaming at the side of her mouth.

Laughing, I turned to check out the edible abs. Blondie had his back to me, but when he turned to the side walking to the next store, I choked on my own spit. From this angle he looked like a spitting image of Lukas. It wasn't until he got close enough that I could see his eyes weren't right, and he lacked Lukas's carefree smile. Breathing again I regained my composure.

"See I told you, but I didn't expect you to get all choked up about it."

"Shut up," I grinned at her after I hacked up a lung over my highly overactive imagination. I was seeing things my subconscious wanted to see.

She smiled back. "Fine, let's do some damage. Where to first?"

"You tell me. You're the one with the bank roll."

"Touché… let's start wherever edible abs is going," she said taking after the Lukas look-a-like.

Tori hauled me to store after store, pillaging through the racks. With an arm loaded with clothes, we made our way into the dressing rooms. Sitting on one those chairs they leave outside the changing rooms; I waited for her to try on the first outfit.

"What's up with you and Gavin?" She called from behind the door.

Thankfully there wasn't anyone else in here with us. "Nothing."

"Really, 'cuz it doesn't seem like a whole lot of nothing," she retorted.

"We're just friends." There was a defensive edge to my

voice.

"Friends my ass," she muffled while pulling on one of the articles of clothing. "That guy looks at you like he's afraid you'll disappear. His eyes are always watching you."

"Whatever, you make it sound creepy," I scoffed.

"I wouldn't call it creepy – intense maybe." She stepped out with a pair of skinny jeans and an off the shoulder tee. She was taller than me and carried it mostly in her legs. Her brown hair was pulled back into a ponytail emphasizing her chocolate eyes. She was quite pretty and I didn't understand why she didn't attract more guys. She surpassed me in the looks department. Her body was pretty killer also, curvy in all the right places and pencil thin.

I glared at her in full pestered disbelief.

"Fine – don't believe me, but I'm serious." She turned in the three-dimensional mirror checking out her butt. "So have you kissed him yet?"

A sigh escaped. "No," I sadly admitted.

"What are you waiting for, an invitation? Gavin is nuts about you. He even rejected Rianne for you," she insisted.

Point well made. There was nothing really standing in the way, which didn't explain why at that moment Lukas came to mind. Was I so enamored by Mr. Dreamy that I was scared by what was right in front of me? Why the hesitation with

Gavin?

"I don't know, maybe you're right," I conceded.

"Of course I'm right. Are you seeing him this weekend?"

We hadn't discussed it, but I kind of assumed we were. "I think…" There was skepticism tracing my words.

"Good, here's your chance." Everything in Tori's mind was so cut and dry. You wanted something – you went for it.

A part of me was being guarded. He was hiding something from me. I felt it. And until I found out what it was, I couldn't take the chance. That didn't mean I didn't want to. But what was the rush?

Five more outfits later and we made our way back into the mall. Packages in hand we strolled to the food court for dinner. I ended up ordering a slice of cheese pizza, and Tori got a taco salad. The great thing about food courts was there was a little something for all taste buds.

After finishing up our calorie lavished meal, we hit a few more stores including Victoria Secret. Picking through a bin of panties and thongs all priced far more than I was willing to pay for such skimpy material, Tori's mind quickly turned to sex. And since she didn't have a current boyfriend, and Austin didn't have a boyfriend, well, I suddenly became the closest thing to sex worthy gossip. Complete shit, because I didn't have the first clue about sex.

"I think you need a pair of these," she declared holding a thong that consisted of three strings and a dangling charm.

"Why would I need those? They look like floss," I sneered.

Swinging them on her finger she sweet-talked. "Because I bet Gavin would love them."

"I think I should take it a little slower... like maybe getting him to kiss me first." I reminded her.

"A girl can never be too prepared. At least that's what my step-mom always says." Tori's step-mom, Mariah wasn't exactly the kind of person I would take advice from. She was twenty some years younger than Tori's dad, and I think this was like her third marriage. I am sure she was prepared for all *kinds* of scenarios.

"Tori my sex life isn't up for discussion. It's nonexistent," I warned.

"Look one of us needs to have sex and since you have a phenomenally hot guy chasing you, it's a sure bet that someone is going to be you. I'm just trying to help out a friend."

I tossed the floss back into the bin. "Thanks for the thought, but no. Besides if we were going to have sex, I'd get these," I replied picking up a purple lacy pair.

She laughed too loud drawing attention our way, and it

was too hard to resist joining her. "I knew it. You want him."

I rolled my eyes. "I'd have to be dead to not want him. I'm just saying we aren't even remotely close to being there."

"Yeah I know, but it's a hell of a lot of fun to talk about."

She had me there.

When I pulled into the driveway, a text message rang in my purse. Unlocking the screen, the message lit the dark interior of the car. It was Gavin, (heartbeat hammering in my chest), inviting me to meet his family tomorrow. Well in his own style.

Come over tomorrow.

I groaned. The idea of seeing his family was scary, but my curiosity overruled the fear.

Sure. I replied.

CHAPTER 9

SATURDAY WAS FRIGHTENING. This was my weekend off from the shop, and I was currently in panic mode. I had changed my outfit at least a dozen times. The evidence littered the floor of my room. Finally, I settled on a pair of skinny denim, a crystal back-tie tank and boots. Primping wasn't my forte. Putting on my usual make-up, I added heavier eyeliner and finished my beauty routine with a sheer lip gloss. I left my auburn hair straight and tumbling down my back. Smacking my lips in the full-length mirror, I sighed. I was out of time, and this was going to have to do.

Only a few blocks down the road from mine, the short drive did very little for my freaked out nerves. I don't know why I felt like a lamb going into the lion's den. Sophie was incredible and Gavin was… well I hadn't figured that out yet. How could his family be anything other than fabulous? *Not scary at all*, I tried to entice.

The Mason household was a fairytale.

The house had recently been repainted in a fresh coat of a soft yellow, trimmed in cottage white. A full wrap-around porch covered the perimeter with a swing gliding on the left. The landscape was alive and vibrant in color; a garden of floral

91

variations weaved about the porch. My aunt would be in pure heaven. Most impressive was the entryway; where two large etched glass paneled doors invited you in. A massive chandelier visible from the outside hung in the foyer, sending a rainbow prism glittering on the glass doors.

Everything about the house made me think of Neverland. You could almost visualize the fairies dancing under moonbeams, with their fluttering fragile wings and childish secretive giggles.

Walking up the short stairs to the porch, I was bombarded with a wave of dizziness. It hit me unaware all at once, and forced me to steady myself on the railing. I was nervous, but this was ridiculous. Once my head cleared, I took a deep breath and rang the doorbell. The crashing of ocean waves sounded from behind the house as I waited.

Sophie answered the door with excitement shinning in her eyes. She pulled me into the house. "I'm so glad you came," she bubbled.

I was lost for words.

Stepping into the grand foyer, the inside was even more startling. Rows of windows flanked the walls on both sides of the foyer. To the left appeared to be a living room with thick plush carpet expanding the room, decorated in hues of turquoises, blues and gold. The room reminded me of feathers on a peacock.

On the right was a study in the works. The immensely fond reader in me sighed in appreciation at the rows upon rows of bookshelves that covered from floor to ceiling. Some filled but many of them waiting to be housed with novels. Boxes of books scattered along the room. It often escaped my mind that the Mason's had moved in just a few weeks ago.

A massive mural was in process overhead on the ceiling. I wasn't able to make out the entire scene from the angle where I stood. What I could see was a portrait of an extraordinary woman with flaming hair like the sky at sundown. She was gracefully posed in her long white dress, whipping out around her. Power emitted from her, through her and about her. She wallowed in her confidence and determination in her stunning eyes.

Directly in front of me stretched an enormous circular staircase. There I notice Gavin's parents waiting to greet us. The staggering beauty of Mrs. Mason struck me speechless. Straight, silky raven hair ran down the length of her back, like Sophie's. She was tall, slender and graced with curves. Something about her heart-shaped face and magnetic cobalt eyes reminded me of mystical Celtic myths. A welcoming smile touched her lips.

At her side was Gavin's father with a light hand on the

small of her back. He was tall and of lean build with sandy brown hair that lay just above his hazel eyes behind horn-rimmed glasses. They were both dressed casually.

"You must be Brianna," his mother greeted in a voice as lovely as her daughter's. She immediately embraced me in yet another hug. Apparently the females in this family were not shy with their affections. I don't think the same could be said for the men, well at least the one I was acquainted with. "I'm Lily and this is John." She gestured to Gavin's father.

"We are so happy to finally meet you," John spoke in a tone timber and male. He smiled my way.

"Thank you. Your home is absolutely beautiful," I complimented.

"It's coming along, still so much to do. Moving is never an easy task." Lily took both my hands in hers. At the touch a blue spark passed between us. I let out a small gasp and raised my startled eyes to hers. She continued with barely an acknowledgement of what we both felt. "Which is why we are so happy that Gavin has met you." Her voice was thick with feeling and sincerity. She was impossible not to adore and did what I hadn't been able to all day – calm my frazzled nerves.

At the mention of his name, Gavin strolled down the spiral staircase. My gaze irrevocably sought his, any calm I felt dissipated. Fireflies tangoed in my belly, and a flush dusted my cheeks. I lost all sense of everything in the room.

"Hey." His husky voice rolled over me, filling me with warmth.

"Hi."

He stood in front of me, and I couldn't think of anything else to say. Had I been acutely aware that I was unabashedly staring, I would have been mortified.

Luckily, Lily filled the silence before it became extremely awkward. "Gavin, why don't you give Brianna a tour," she suggested, breaking the thick contact permeating the air. "I'm going to finish dinner with Sophie's help," she said turning to her daughter.

"But I was going to show Brianna around," Sophie protested.

"I think Gavin can handle it." Lily glanced back at me. She had such an air of maternal instinct about her. "Brianna we would love for you to stay for dinner, Sophie especially." Her smile only brightened her features.

"Sure, thanks," I replied.

"Come on," Gavin said, lacing his fingers with mine. "Let's go before Sophie swindles her way out of kitchen duty."

I had already seen most of the main floor with the open layout the house had, so he took me up the winding staircase.

"This is Sophie's." He indicated to the first room on the

95

left.

Her room was bohemian chic. A wrought-iron bed stood in the center of the room draped with bold jewel-toned bedding. A crystal embellished teal canopy tailored the corners of her bed. It felt like walking into a gypsy camp.

Down the hall and to the right we came to another bedroom.

"Jared should be here shortly. This is his." His voice was like music to my ears. I was pretty sure I could listen to him ramble about the news, and I would be enamored.

Messy summed up Jared's room in one word. The room looked and smelled like a fraternity.

Our hands were still joined as he led me around. I loved the feeling of our entwined fingers. I wasn't willing to give up his, any time soon. There was an underlying spark of awareness.

"And this one is mine." He walked into the room angled at the end of the hall.

Gavin's room wasn't at all what I expected. I figured he'd have black walls and heavy metal posters, which made no sense since he didn't actually listen to heavy metal. His room was much neater than Jared's to my great pleasure. He did have a black framed bed with a book shelf as the headboard lined with black and white photos. A large stereo and TV housed with CDs, DVDs and an Xbox sat across the bed. The scent of him was everywhere – taunting me.

It felt naughty being alone in his room. Not like the time we spent in mine. This was suddenly more intimate.

"Let me show you the best part." He led the way to a set of French doors. They opened to a circular balcony with a spectacular view of the ocean just steps from the house.

I leaned over the railings and inhaled the fresh air of the evening tide. "This is amazing," I said in awe. "To wake up to this view every morning…" My voice trailed off, taken by the crashing waves.

"You want to check it out?" he asked with excitement. Clearly he appreciated the sea as much as I did.

I nodded my head.

While we waited for dinner he took me for a walk along the ocean's rocky shoreline. "What do your parents do?" I had removed my shoes earlier, and my feet buried in the sand as we walked.

"My dad is a historian, and my mom is an artist," he answered.

"Did she paint the mural in the library?" I looked up into his face. Our arms swung together as we strolled on the beach.

"She did. It's not quite done yet," he explained. "She

paints a lot of mythology and folklore."

"It's stunning," I praised. Stopping, I bent down to grab a glittering shell that caught my eye.

He looked out into the indigo vastness of the ocean. The sun was setting, casting an assortment of oranges and purples at the horizon.

"It's a depiction of Morgana le Fey." His glance returned to me. "She reminds me of you."

I snorted, "You're kidding right? That painting was beautiful."

Nibbling on his lip ring he considered what I said, looking sinful and serious. "So are you." His tone had lowered.

I swear I heard him wrong. Maybe that was just what I wanted to hear. Right then I wanted more than anything for him to kiss me, with the lapping waves and sea salt teasing my wits. Maybe if I thought about it hard enough I could somehow have what my heart desired.

He took a step closer. The heat from his body infused mine, and a sharp gasp escaped my lips. My head was lost on a turbulent of raw emotions. *Kiss me now*, my mind demanded.

The depths of his eyes darkened, and his mouth crushed over my mine in an assault of power. Excitement rippled inside me like chain lightening. His hands gripped my sides, pulling me in and steadying my swirling head all at once. He tasted of dark promises and pleasure beyond what I could imagine. Filling my entire being with flames, I encircled my arms around his neck. With nothing between us our bodies collided. My mouth traveled lavishly over his, loving the feel of his cool hoop rubbing against mine.

As first kisses went, this was unworldly. The flavor of him was an addiction I wasn't able to fulfill. He made me dizzy, weak and feel exactly what he claimed – beautiful.

The kiss ended to my utter dismay, as fast as it began. He pulled away, keeping me at arm's length. I moaned at the loss of his lips and opened my eyes. Gavin gazed longingly at my swollen mouth before shutting his eyes again. He laid his brow on mine, and I breathed the familiar scent of him mixing with the misty spray. Our quickened breathing synchronized in heavy rhythm.

Dropping his hands from my lower arms, he broke the spell. "We better get back inside." His voice was thick with huskiness.

I had to fight every muscle in my body not to pull his mouth back to mine. His self-control was staggering, which was both annoying and honorable.

I nodded. No longer touching, we turned back towards the house. The slow walk back allowed me barely enough time to control my thrashing heart.

As we got closer to the kitchen I heard a slew of animated voices bantering back and forth. Gavin and I stepped into the dining nook where I was greeted with smells of spaghetti sauce and garlic. My stomach rumbled in response. I hadn't had an appetite earlier, and my stomach was in serious protest. The remaining of his family was gathered, including the brother I yet to meet.

A hush fell over the room as we stepped in. Sophie smiled beside her eldest brother.

"Jared this is Brianna. Be nice," Sophie warned him.

A laugh snickered from his chest, and a wolfish grin spread across his face, looking similar to Gavin's, but without the seriousness. He had a boyish charm, the devils smile and irresistible dimples. Jared pulled out his chair and walked to stand in front of me, smiling the entire time.

"It's a pleasure to meet you beautiful Brianna." His voice almost as seductive as his brothers, but it failed to send my heart sputtering in overdrive. Instead his smile was contagious, and I found myself answering his devilish grin.

"You too," I said, my voice having yet to recover from the emotional onslaught.

"Here I saved you a seat." He pulled out a chair beside him.

Gavin growled and eyes darkened, brewing with a

violent storm.

"Jared," Lily warned in a stern tone. I wasn't exactly sure what was going on, but Gavin was not happy. There was a thick static in the air, suffocating the room. No one else seemed to notice, but I knew they felt it.

"What?" he answered in mischievous laugh. "I'm just being gracious," he defended with charisma.

Dinner was delicious, and it felt so inviting being included in a family dinner. It was so full of commotion, laughter, and so opposite of my own dinners at home. I never realized what I was missing in not having a large family.

"It's Saturday night. Let's go out," Gavin suggested over the chatter.

"There must be a bowling alley or something in this town," Jared added in exasperation to my left. He didn't seem like the kind of soul to sit idly around. He screamed action.

"Yeah there is, but –" I was cut off.

"Great. Let's get out of here," Jared swiftly interrupted my rebuttal.

I royally sucked at bowling. Gutters were the only thing my ball hit.

CHAPTER 10

HOLLY RIDGE BOWL WAS NO sight to behold. There were ten bowling lanes, a small arcade and a bar in the corner that served only beer and frozen pizzas. As we walked through the alley only two of the lanes were currently occupied. I could not believe that I had let them talk me into this. It was going to be so humiliating.

The four of us went up to the register, and Jared requested a lane.

"We should play on teams," he suggested. "A little competition, what do you say." There was a gleam in his eyes.

"Jared and I against Gavin and Brianna," Sophie recommended.

Gavin turned to me. "You okay with that?" he asked grinning. I knew he could see my discomfort.

"Sure," I agreed. "It's your loss," I mumbled under my breath.

"Have a little faith Bri. With me by your side, we can't lose," he assured me with too much confidence.

"We'll see little brother," Jared countered loving the banter.

We gave the guy behind the register our shoe sizes and

set off for lane six.

"Any chance we're using bumpers?" I asked as we wound our way down.

Jared laughed, but I wasn't being funny. I would have totally used bumpers.

"Not a chance," Jared replied still grinning. "Trust me. We won't need them the way we bowl."

Great. Was that supposed to make me feel better? What were they, bowling fanatics? I had no idea what the heck I had gotten myself into. "Lovely," I retorted sarcastically.

I set off in search for the lightest ball possible. Maybe they would let me just watch? Picking up a few of the bowling balls, testing their weight I resignedly decided on a blue seven pounder.

At least it was a pretty color.

Sophie was setting up the order into the computer when I came back with my sparkling blue ball. I took a seat next to her and waited dreadfully for my turn.

"Thanks for coming with us," Sophie said next to me. "This is the first time we've really been out since we moved here."

Her words penetrated the wall of dismay I had going, making me feel remorseful for wallowing in self-pity. They were new in this town. I should be making them feel

103

welcomed.

"Sure, no problem." I attempted to muster up some enthusiasm.

Jared was the first one up, and in perfect form threw a strike. There was no doubt in my mind. I was going to get slaughtered. He strutted off the lane giving Sophie a high-five as he took his seat.

Gavin was up next. He looked adorable in his t-shirt, black jeans and the multi-colored block bowling shoes. Keeping with the theme the Mason family had going, he of course threw a strike. This was going to be a long game, I thought miserably.

Being the good sport that I am, I grinned at my partner on his way back to our seats. "Nice work. At least one of us will score points."

He sat beside me smirking. "It's all in fun."

"Wait until you see me bowl," I said somberly.

Sophie at least didn't get a strike. She knocked eight of the pins the first time and on the second wasn't able to pick them up.

It was a nasty split.

"Your turn Brianna," Sophie called after her last throw.

"Here goes nothing." Literally.

I walked up to the lane and grabbed my blue ball.

Fitting my fingers in the holes, I aligned my feet with the triangles on the floor. With a quick prayer, I sent the ball sailing down the lane. Halfway it started to curve, riding on the line. I backed up afraid to look, but even more afraid not to. A lonely crack sounded as the ball knocked over only one pin. My shoulders sagged a little.

"At least you have great form," Jared razzed.

He was rewarded with a punch in the arm from Gavin.

"What?" He pretended innocence then winked at me while I waiting for the ball to be retrieved.

My next throw was slightly better. I was able to take down three more pins.

"Don't let them get to you," Sophie encouraged as I sat down next to her. "It's really just a brotherly competition, a power struggle between the two of them. I don't know why they enjoy it so much."

"Are they always like this?"

She nodded her head. "They are forever trying to outdo each other but not aggressively. It's all in fun, as frustrating as it is for the rest of us."

"Yeah… I can see that," I agreed.

"It's so nice to have another girl around. I'm always caught in the crossfire. You balance the scales now."

"I'm not all that graceful," I jested.

"You are a lot of things you don't believe." There was a prophetic knowledge behind her words. As friends went, Sophie was pretty uplifting to have around.

My next few turns where no better. Actually they were worse.

Gavin leaned in closer beside me. "Let me give you a tip. Think about what you want the ball to do, visualize it before you throw and keep the image as you release. Works for me every time," he swore grinning.

"You're joking," I said in disbelief.

He lifted his brow.

"Fine."

My next turn, I thought, what could it hurt, and gave it a shot. I did exactly what he'd said. I envisioned the ball gliding down the middle of the lane, hitting it dead center. Ignoring everything I thought I knew about bowling, I let the ball soar down the lane. Not expecting much as the ball thundered the pins, I was stupefied when all the white pins fell.

I jumped in the air and bounded down the lane straight into Gavin's arms. He twirled me once before setting me back on my feet.

"See, I knew you could do it," he cheered.

"Beginners luck," Jared joked beside me.

I stuck my tongue out at him, and he hooted with

laughter.

The strikes kept on coming, and the competition never let up. Something about the way they played struck a chord with me. I started to *really* pay attention. No one was that good, not without some help, my skeptical mind rationed. It wasn't the way they bowled or their form. What made me leery were their eyes.

Each time Gavin or Jared bowled they would line up and eye the pins. It was then that I noticed the bizarre glow in them, the same glow I saw at the coffee shop. Before they released their throw, the gleam shined brightly. Over the last few frames I came to expect to see it. I considered it to be a trick of lighting, but the moment Sophie went to bowl, her eyes remained the same. No glint, no glimmer, no unearthly glow.

When the night ended Gavin offered to drive me home. We had dropped my car off earlier on the way. The prices of gas were outrageous, and I needed to save a buck where I could.

The night was late, and the moon was mostly hidden. Gavin's shadowy form was outlined by the neon blue of his interior lights. I shifted in the leather seat laying my head on the back of the headrest, watching him.

This was the first time we had been alone since we kissed earlier, and I wasn't really sure what to say. So of course

I complicated matters by saying what had been on my mind the better half of the night. A part of me thought I was making a gigantic mistake by bringing it up. He could very well think that I was a lunatic. I didn't want to admit how much that would hurt, but I knew that there was no way I was going to let this go, especially if there was an off chance that I was right.

"You're different." My quiet voice broke the silence through the steady purr of his engine.

"What do you mean?" He had both eyes still on the road, but I knew he wanted to look at me. His jaw tightened ever so slightly.

"I don't know, just different." I had such a way with words It was uncanny.

"Different how?" he asked, his voice had stiffened, and I knew I hit a nerve.

Heaving a heavy sigh, "I just feel it. That you are something else –" I explained warily. He gave in and looked at me with a perplexed expression. "Tonight... I saw your eyes glow. Jared's also. I've seen it before." I rushed the end of the confession – absurd as it was. "What are you?" I asked.

Cutting his gaze back to the road, he was silent. "I've been too relaxed with you," he mumbled, chastising himself. Or at least that is what I thought I heard.

"Are you a werewolf or something?" I was only half

teasing. Though a part of me actually thought he might just be a werewolf.

"Bri do you really think that I turn into a wolf and howl at the moon, or that I am any different than you?"

I bite my lip. "I don't know," I admitted, more unsure than ever.

"I'm not," he said seriously.

It was hard not to believe him. Maybe this whole thing was just me. Maybe I was the one who wasn't *normal*. Right now I didn't even know what that meant. We didn't talk at all the remaining way home, each caught in our own thoughts.

When he pulled up to my house, I hadn't the first clue how to undo the tension. "Gavin –"

He cut me off. "Bri just let it go." He tried to sound lighthearted but failed. I could still hear the strain in his tone. "I'll talk to you tomorrow."

I nodded and got out of the car without another word, no matter that I had a hundred more questions and an apology I badly wanted to utter at the tip of my tongue.

Later that night I laid spread on the bed, my hands propped under my chin and feet dangling in the air. The television was on low while I artlessly riffled through the channels, not really paying attention to the screen.

I was mentally trying to dissect the puzzle of Gavin and

his family or the possibility it was all me. There was the crazy way I felt about him. He caused elevated emotions, and I was drawn to him in an irrevocable pull, both terrifying and confounding. Uncontrollably compelled by him, I was taken in by the sultry sapphire of his eyes.

Then there was humming vibration I sometimes got when he or Sophie touched me. Or the strange light of his and Jared eyes, like at the coffee shop or tonight. He might want me to drop the suspicion, yet my mind was having a difficult time of it.

How had I let any of this happen? It was stupid – absolutely stupid to fall for someone like Gavin. He could be so grating and his smirk infuriating. Those seemed petty and insignificant excuses compared to the sputter of my rapid heartbeat. He made my head spin and left me feeling breathless when we were together.

I fell asleep with the television flicking in the background, the barely audible voices drifting with me in dreams. And like most of my dreams, they were of Lukas, a detail that ate at my guilt. When seconds before all I could imagine was Gavin. How messed up was that?

CHAPTER 11

"I MISSED YOU," HE SAID as soon as he saw me. We were in a park, sitting on a marble bench. There was an elaborate stone fountain bubbling at the heart. Robins and blue jays sang from the treetops, chasing each other through the branches.

"Me too," I agreed. I had really missed him.

"We've seen more of each other the last few weeks than we have… ever," he commented about my increased number of dreams.

Yeah we had. Why was that?

I shrugged. "Who knows how my mind works."

He laughed and put an arm around the back of the bench, encompassing me in his nearness. "I like the way your mind works." Grinning he inched closer. He was wearing khaki shorts and a polo tee. The air outside was comfortable and sunny. A flock of robins picked at the grass in front of us.

If I didn't know better the golden boy was flirting with me. "That's just sad," I retorted, unable to believe anyone liked my mind.

He laughed. "Oh Brianna, when will you see what I see?"

I had no idea what he saw, but I didn't think in the *real* world it would make a difference. "I think you need to get your eyes checked," I suggested offhandedly.

He ignored my comment. "So have you seen the new guy?" He tried to sound nonchalant, but I could hear the underlying disapproval.

"It's hard not to. We have a class together." I was a little annoyed by the fact that he brought up Gavin. There was an accusation that rubbed me the wrong way.

A warning.

A screaming of caution.

"Does that bother you?" I absently kicked the dust under the bench.

"I'm just curious about him."

Oh it seemed like a whole lot more than just curiosity bubbled under the surface. Didn't anyone ever tell him that curiosity killed the cat? "Why?" I couldn't resist questioning him to prove it was more.

He gazed out into the park at an aging statue of a horse with a warrior on its back. "I can see the he means something to you," he finally admitted.

How was I to respond to that when I wasn't even sure what I was feeling? He was accurate that Gavin meant something to me, but it wasn't any of his business. And how exactly did he know that? Because I thought about him when I was here with Lukas? My brows muddled in confusion. I couldn't deny my feelings for Gavin and lying sounded like a bad idea. If he could tell that I cared about Gavin, then it was a good guess he could tell if I lied.

"We're friends." I was trying to be evasive.

"I can make you forget him," he pledged. His emerald eyes locked with mine, and he saw the stunned expression on my face. I didn't want to forget Gavin, but that didn't stop him from taking full advantage of my speechless shock.

He leaned towards me and pressed his mouth lightly to mine. And I let him.

I didn't pull away.

I didn't stop him.

If anything I wanted it.

This kiss was a chance I'd wondered about too often to let slip away.

His lips were soft, smooth and dreamy. They moved expertly over mine, drawing out each heavenly sensation and causing me to forget any doubts. The tips of his fingers moved lazily on the small of my back, gently coaxing me closer. He tasted of golden honey and sugary spice. Degree by slow degree I submerged into the kiss, letting it carry me to ecstasy. He cupped the sides of my face, his hands tender, keeping us locked together. His thumb stroked my cheek affectionately. He made my head feel like it was flying with the clouds. Floating on desire that felt endless, the kiss was perfect and sweet.

Perfect except that it lacked the punch my kiss with Gavin had, or the passionate desperation – like my last breath depended on him. Lukas's kiss was sweet, compassionate and wistful. I've been kissed twice in one evening, and they were on irreconcilable planes of the spectrum. Not to mention this was a dream, but it felt just as real.

I knew that just as sure as this kiss would end, I would feel overwhelming guilt. His lips left mine lingeringly and his pure green eyes opened slowly. He kept our faces close and traced a feather soft finger over my thoroughly kissed lips.

"I've wanted to do that for so long," he murmured low. "Something for you to think about," he said, his voice like honey silk.

I didn't need anything else to think about. The dream started to drift away slowly. I could feel myself being sucked back into my sleeping form. His emerald eyes and the sunny scent of him wafted with me.

Before I was completely tossed out, a woman's raspy voice slipped in through the journey. "Be careful what you trust. Dreams aren't always what they seem," she warned, her voice fading off in the distance.

When I woke up in my darkened room, the taste of his honey smooth lips lingered on mine. My body was humming and alive. I lay there the rest of the night feeling exactly what I predicted I would. Guilt. The woman's voice and her warning were long forgotten.

***

When I got to school on Monday, I was in a zombie-like state. Yawning endlessly, my eyes were heavy like there were weights on them. The extra effort it took to keep them open proved to be too much during first period when I feel asleep on my desk.

Mrs. Schwab's voice echoed in ears before I fully realized that she wasn't talking in my head.

"Brianna… Brianna… would you like to join the class?"

Wiping the drool with the back of my hand, I inclined my head towards her voice. "Sorry," I barely managed to mumble.

She eyed me with disdain. Turning her back on me, she continued her lecture. Austin caught my attention a row over and gave me a, *what the hell* look. I sighed, and my shoulders slumped in exhaustion.

He walked out with me after class. "Hey babygirl. Is

that hot piece of boy candy keeping you up at night?"

I snickered. "Not exactly."

"You okay?" he asked with a touch of worry.

"I haven't a clue. Just tired I think."

"We're still on for Friday right?" he asked, reminding me of our plans.

Friday was Halloween night. Tori, Austin, Gavin, Sophie and I planned on going out. It was all Austin's idea. I loved Halloween. We were going to the Haunted Trails at Morris Landing. Sophie, Tori and I even decided to dress up. The three of us were getting together later this week to shop for our costumes. Gavin's badass claimed he didn't need a costume. Whatever. What fun was that?

"Yeah of course. I am so excited," I assured.

"I know. It's going to be a scream," he lamely attempted in humor.

I usually laughed at even Austin's bad jokes. Today I couldn't even accomplish that. "Funny," I replied.

"See you at lunch," he called as we broke off in different directions.

By the time third period hit, I was finishing my second cup of coffee hoping for an adrenaline boost. Gavin caught up with me as I topped off the last of my caffeine and tossed the evidence in the trash. He arched his brow lifting the silver bar in query.

"Why so glum?" he inquired.

A yawn escaped the second I opened mouth. "There is something wrong with me. I shouldn't be so tired after the amount of caffeine I just inhaled," I admitted.

He studied my face as we walked. "Didn't sleep well?"

I shook my head, stifling another yawn "No that's what's weird. I slept all night. I shouldn't be this tired." Neither of us mentioned the previous night or what I had accused him of. I was too tired to even care at this point and was glad I couldn't detect any weird tension.

"Maybe it's your dreams," he suggested. "Especially if they're of me. I could see how that could be disrupting."

I choked on his words. "Maybe," I conceded thinking about the dream I had of Lukas and the kiss we shared. *God if he only knew*, I thought in embarrassment. Better yet I was glad he didn't.

"They're probably keeping you up."

"You're probably right," I agreed, starting to get a little uncomfortable with this topic. I didn't want to talk about Lukas with Gavin.

I started thinking about Gavin and I. What I couldn't figure out was why Gavin had picked me from all the girls at this school. Surely I wasn't his first choice. What was so special about me? He'd said that once to me. Maybe some of Sophie's abrasiveness was rubbing off on me. It was the only excuse I had for blurting out my thoughts.

"Why did you pick me?"

"What do you mean?" he replied and stopped walking.

This wasn't going to go well. Why couldn't I just let things be? We were in a good place after last night it seemed, why did I have to go and put tautness between us again? I thought maybe I was trying to sabotage whatever we had going on purpose. "There are hundreds of girls in this school, why did you pick me?" I repeated. A few students passing by on their way to class glanced our way.

"Why is it so hard for you to believe?" He raised his voice an octave.

He answered a question with a question, which was so nerve racking. I shrugged, feeling more exposed than I thought possible and defeated. What kind of admission had I been expecting? That he was madly in love with me and couldn't live without me?

"It just is," I argued.

He ran a frustrated hand through his midnight hair, the leather cuff on his wrist slid with the movement. "We have something in common," he finally admitted.

"What?" I asked taken by surprise and even though I

wasn't expecting a declaration of love, my heart faltered a tad.

"Isn't it enough that I am attracted to you?" He disputed evasively.

I don't know, was it? His words affected me, giving me a river of thrilled sensation. I stared at his eyes, waiting to see some form of deceit. They were clear, blue and honest. The bell sounded through the hall announcing the beginning of third period. For now it would have to be enough because we were both late for class, and I was too exhausted to continue.

I don't know how I made it through the whole day. But as soon as last period ended I went home and slept like the dead.

Dreamless.

CHAPTER 12

AFTER SCHOOL THE NEXT DAY, Gavin came over to study for our chemistry group test we had the following day. By group test, I meant Gavin and me. While I planned on studying, Gavin had another idea entirely. Honestly I would have preferred to study without him sitting across the bed from me. He was a distraction from even the simplest thoughts, let alone a chapter of science that didn't make a lick of sense. But he had asked me and I had yet to refuse him anything.

I had the textbook open and a spiral notebook with bare minimum notes spread out around us on the bed. Biting the end of my pencil, I flipped through our study guide Mr. Burke had given us. It outlined the points in the chapter that we would be tested on.

"Are we really going to study?" he asked complaining.

"Yes," I replied exasperated. "I have to pass this class. So do you."

He grumbled beside me, doodling on the notebook.

I yanked it out from underneath his pen. "Hey," he protested. "I wasn't finished with that."

"Chemistry remember… we are supposed to be studying."

"You are a slave driver," he stated, fumbling with his pen cap.

"You are a slacker," I contradicted.

"Ouch. Can't we take a break?" He was bordering on whining, and I felt like I was babysitting a two year old.

I laughed. "We just started. Here look up question ten in the text." Hoping that giving something to do would get him involved. I peered at him over the top of our study guide. He was flipping through the pages of our textbook looking sexy as sin. It was hard to believe that he was here in my room with me. When I imagined dating, I never pictured someone like him – dark, edgy, or with so many piercings. But now that there was a chance that maybe we could date, I didn't want any other boy at my school. He ruined all other prospects for me.

Yesterday's tizzy in the hall was forgotten. We couldn't seem to stay upset with each other and easily forgave our snags. The snags seemed to be me mostly my issue.

Biting the end of my eraser, he looked up and caught me ogling him. Of course my cheeks stained pink, he smirked, and I quickly went back to our study guide. Now my concentration was shot to hell.

"You're not studying," he playfully scolded.

I kicked him lightly from across the bed. He grabbed ahold of my leg before I had the chance to escape his reach.

"Hey!" I screeched.

"Just remember that you started it." He pulled me by the leg towards him. I was laughing and squealing at the same time. As soon as he had me in his grasp, he picked me up effortlessly and tossed me to the other end of the bed on a pile of pillows. My laughter peeled out over the silence of the empty house, so much for studying.

Sometime later I looked over at the clock on my nightstand. My stomach rumbled in response as I thought about dinner. My aunt wasn't due home for a few more hours, and it was my turn to cook. Even with her gone most of the time, she insisted on trying to make sure I had a balanced diet and was well taken care of. I know how much it grated on her that I was alone some much. On her nights, she usually had something in the fridge ready to be cooked or a cold pasta salad.

Tonight the menu was Italian.

"I'm starving." My stomach protested with my admission. "Do you want to stay for dinner? I'm making lasagna." I didn't really want to eat alone, and there was always so much, no matter how many nights I ate leftovers.

"You're cooking?" he asked and scrunched his nose.

I tossed my pencil good-naturedly at him. "I'm a good cook, I'll have you know."

He caught the pencil mid-air before it had a chance to

hit its target and smirked at me. "Sure, under one condition," he countered.

"What?" I replied narrowing my eyes cautiously.

"You let me help."

"Deal. Let's go before I pass out from hunger," I said grinning and climbed off my bed, the litter of notes forgotten.

We walked into the kitchen, and I preheated the oven. Going to the pantry I started to pull out what I needed, pasta sauce, noodles and spices.

"What do you want me to do?" he asked behind me seated at the island in the middle of our kitchen.

"You can make the salad," I instructed, setting down the stuff from the pantry, I went to the fridge. Pulling out the hamburger and vegetables I placed them on the counter. I handed him a knife from the butcher block. "Can you handle this?"

He lifted his brow. "You haven't seen anything."

I went back to the stove, put the hamburger in a pan and set a pot of water to boil. Turning on the burner, I began breaking apart the ground beef and browning it. Looking over my shoulder I checked to see how he was doing chopping the salad.

"You did not just cut up all the vegetables," I declared, mystified by the impossible. There was no way in the time that

I had turned my back he could have made an entire salad.

"I told you not to doubt me," he said grinning, so sure of himself.

"What are you a chef? You're practically failing chemistry, yet you can create a salad in under a minute. What gives?"

"Talent. Do you need help over there?"

"Yeah, boil the noodles smarty pants."

We worked together in a seamless rhythm. It was like harmony and completely domestic. There was something so homey about having him in the kitchen with me. Maybe it was from growing up without a male figure or maybe it was that he was so familiar with cooking, either way it was nice to not be alone. Cooking for two was not only boring and lonely but lacked the sense of family I missed out on. With the lasagna baking in the oven, we sat at the table, kicked back with the radio on low.

"Where did you move from?" I asked wondering lately where he came from.

"We lived just outside of Chicago, until my dad got the job offer in Jacksonville."

I was surprised. I didn't know how many job opportunities there were for a historian. Let alone exactly what a historian did.

"What was it like there?"

"Busy. Windy. Cold." He grinned.

I rolled my eyes. Those were all things I already knew about Chicago. "Do you miss your old friends?" I asked, secretly wondering if he also had an ex-girlfriend there as well.

He slouched back in his seat and smiled. His whole face relaxed "Yes, sometimes I do. Chicago was where I was born. It was really hard to leave. My friends understood me in ways people here won't be able to." His smile drooped, and he looked a little lost in the past.

My heart went out to him, I couldn't even think about leaving Holly Ridge. Starting over somewhere foreign, making new friends, for the socially awkward like me that sounded disastrous. But there was no denying how glad I was that he was here with me instead of in Chicago were we would have never met.

The buzzer sounded on the oven pulling us each from our own thoughts. Dinner was done. Getting up I dished out our plates and brought them to the table. It was so strange having a guy over for dinner – just the two of us. If I wasn't careful this was something that I could get use to and want more of. Time alone with him.

"What makes the people so different here?" I had to ask. And did that include me?

He shrugged, forking a heap of lasagna into his mouth. "Culture I guess, except you. I felt a connection with you the first day we meet. I remember thinking, *finally someone who will get me*."

I bit into my garlic bread and thought about the first time I saw him. Maybe I judged him too harshly that day for skipping out on class. I never really thought about what he was going through being the *new* kid. Or what he had to leave behind. My heart beat a little faster at his admission of the connection we both felt.

"Is that why you ditched on your first day?" I blew at a bite of steaming lasagna before putting it into my mouth.

"Partly," he admitted. "Mostly I was pissed at my parents, but running into you that day changed my mind about small towns. It's one of the reasons my mom was so happy we met, helping her angry son make the new town slightly more bearable. You wouldn't have recognized me had you seen me before that day. I was rebelling every way possible. I don't think my mom could've thanked you enough. She absolutely adores you," he said polishing off his plate in record time.

The feeling was completely mutual. "I'm sorry it was hard for you. I can't imagine leaving the only home I've ever known."

"Surprisingly I think it worked out for the best. I never

would have thought."

When we finished dinner, I walked him to the door. "Thanks for staying."

"Anytime," he agreed.

"You know that we are going to fail that test tomorrow," I told him. Group test or not we were doomed.

"Have a little faith Bri. I'll get us through it," he smugly assured me.

I rolled my eyes and shut the door after him.

CHAPTER 13

MADAME CORA'S WARDROBE WAS A costume establishment packed with plenty of flair in Wilmington. Austin decided to tag along for the thirty minute trip and was riding shotgun with Sophie and I in the back. Tori convinced him that it would be fun if they dress-up as a pair.

Both Tori and Austin had adopted Sophie instantaneously. They absolutely loved her. I think that grated on Gavin's nerves a tad, to have his younger sister hanging around all the time.

Walking into Madame Cora's Wardrobe was like being transported back in time. A tall woman with long curly cinnamon hair sat on a stool behind an enclosed glass case. She was decorated in more dangling silver jewelry than I thought one woman should wear. Or own. Her every move jingled in music. She had bold red lips – an extreme contrast to her ivory skin and hazel eyes. She smiled at us as we walked through the front door, a whimsical chime resounding through the shop announcing our arrival.

The shop had mannequins dressed up in full gear – wigs, shoes, make-up, masks. You name it, she had it. I saw Jack Sparrow, Medusa, Queen of the Nile, the guy from Saw.

He still gave me nightmares. A Halloween mix pumped in the store from speakers near the doors.

"Well hello my lovelies," she greeted in a voice of a seductress. I don't know who she thought she was going to seduce since Austin was the only guy, and he definitely didn't swing her curvy way.

"Hi." The four of us said in unison.

"Is there something I can help you look for," she offered, never losing the deep sexy quality to her voice.

We had started to peruse around the store, poking through the racks near the entrance. "We're looking for Halloween costumes," Sophie spoke for the group. She eyed Madame Cora coolly, measuring her with bright sapphire eyes. There was just a hint of that strange glow.

Round racks housed costumes of variety. Sexy. Scary. Slutty. The three S's. She had it all. The best part was the quality of the materials. They weren't the cheap mass produced ones you found at Wal-Mart. The detail was spectacularly crafted. I found the most difficult part of shopping here was going to be which costume to choose.

"If you need any help, you let me know," she offered, returning Sophie's inspection. Her blood red nails taped on the glass.

Tori and Austin took off to a row on the back wall filled

with companion costumes, while Sophie and I stayed at the center racks.

"Do you have an idea what you want to dress up as?" I asked Sophie, pulling out a black cat outfit. So not my style, I put it back in with the others.

"I haven't dressed up since junior high." That was only two years ago, but I figured she didn't need me to point that out. "I don't know maybe a French maid or a fairy," she suggested, pulling out an extremely short and barely there black and white skirt with a matching, even smaller, top.

I couldn't really see her as either. "That is pretty darn short," I commented as she held up the skirt. I am sure she would look freaking amazing in anything she wore with those legs.

"I know... that's the point right? The chance to dress slutty without the usually backlash," she pointed out.

She had me there. I wasn't so sure her brothers would agree, but since I didn't have any... "You think Jared and Gavin would let you wear that?" I was trying to rationalize a potential situation. They were both overly protective of Sophie as much as they teased her.

She snorted. "Please. My brother has a thing for you, he could care less what I wear. He will be too busy looking at you," Sophie said offhandedly. She was wrestling through a rack of angel costumes. Sophie was a get-to-the-point kind of girl. No beating around the bush.

"Excuse me." She completely caught me off guard. I was not entirely comfortable with her banking on him being too distracted by me. She couldn't possibly be serious.

"Gavin," she responded grinning at my growing discomfort.

I kind of figured that part out, Captain Obvious. "Define *thing*."

"He is totally into you," she said astonished by my cluelessness.

"Really?" The disbelief was thick in my tone. Okay so we kissed once and we did hang out a lot but it was impossible to believe that he felt even half of the way I did.

She rolled her eyes, the ones identical to the brother in question. "You have no idea the amount of power you have there, do you? We really need to have a girl-to-girl talk."

Okay this was her brother we were discussing; she was not my first choice girl to chat about my womanly wiles with. Or lack of in my case. Plus it was sad that she apparently had more experience in this department than I did. "I don't have any *power* over your brother," I argued.

She rolled her eyes. "Here, wear this one." She handed me a revealing gypsy costume. The skirt was violet with an

131

extremely large slit up the leg. It would probably show more skin than I was at ease with. There was a wrapper bejeweled with chattering gold coins. The top was white with flared sleeves and showed a little midriff.

"You're kidding right?"

"Absolutely not. This is the one," she insisted.

I did really like it. What the hell. The goal was to be someone else. Well I wanted to be hot. Smokin' hot. And this number was sizzling.

Sophie settled for a skanky angel outfit, which in my mind kind of defeated the point of being an angel. Tori and Austin, the nuts that they were, decided to go as Brad and Janet from *Rocky Horror Picture Show*. The best Halloween musical ever.

Yeah, I was that girl.

I was the last in line as I waited to pay. Laying down the gypsy costume near the register, I waited for Madame Cora. Well I assumed that's who she was. Glancing into the glass encasement I admired the jewelry. She had so many beautiful pieces with raw cut stones and silvery charms. While I was admiring a certain necklace that had caught my eye, Madame Cora had come to stand on the other side of the counter.

"Do you dabble in crystals?" she asked me.

I shook my head. "No. I just think they are pretty."

"No... hmmm, I would have thought you did," she admitted looking at me oddly.

I don't know what made her think that I knew anything about crystals and magic.

"Here, let me show you. Each has its own unique properties. This one here —" She indicated to the bauble around her neck. "Is for clear sight and open mindedness." Her voice enthralled me.

She unlocked the glass case, pulling out an intricate silver chain with a rainbow milky stone and a purple crystal. My eyes were spellbound by the necklace that I had only moments before been intrigued by. I don't know how she figured it was that specific piece I was interested in. My fingers itched to touch the smooth stones. They weren't raw cut like some of the others, but flat and polished. She laid it on the counter, and I ran my fingers over the crystals.

"This one is made of moonstone and amethyst," she informed. "The moonstone is said to strengthen intuitive power. Placed under a pillow, alongside an amethyst, can allow for a more peaceful sleep. The amethyst protects against evil sorcery. Something tells me you are in need of some."

I picked up the necklace and let it twirl from my finger. The stones glinted off the lights overhead. Her words affected some deep part of me, locked away. I knew that this necklace was made for me. I didn't know if it was just coincidence that the properties of the stones were incorporated so close to my life. I was starting to believe that I should leave nothing to chance.

So, of course, I added it to my purchase. Not to mention, it would look great with my costume.

She rang up my items and handed me my bags. A tingling shot down my arm as our fingers touched. It was more commanding than what I had gotten accustomed to with Gavin and Sophie. Her hand snaked out and grabbed my arm, holding me. I lifted my head and saw the eerie glow in her eyes, almost like she was possessed. A gasp escaped my lips, and I tugged at my arm. Before I really had the chance to feel freaked out beyond my control, Sophie was by my side.

"Ready?" she asked staring intently at Madame creepo. She was giving her the stink eye.

Madame Cora released my arm at Sophie's immediate response. I couldn't have been more grateful. "Yeah let's go," I swiftly agreed.

"May safety find you…Brianna," Madame Cora called as we walked out of the store.

Once we were in the car, I allowed myself to breathe. That woman had touched some secret part of me that was partially intrigued and partially horrified.

"That was weird," Austin commented as Tori started reversing out of the parking space.

"No kidding," Tori agreed. "I guess Halloween started a little early for some. Or maybe never ends in her case."

Sophie and I sat in silence. I had taken the necklace out of the bag and was absently fingering the stones. Sophie occasionally eyed me wearily. I knew she was checking to make sure I was okay, that I wasn't crept out by what happened. In truth I didn't know what to make of it.

CHAPTER 14

HALLOWEEN NIGHT WAS MY FAVORITE. The moonlit air was infused with the scent of damp leaves and wet moss. Fall had moved in like an artist's brush, painting the trees in vibrant colors of gold, burgundy, rust and tangerine. I stood on my porch dressed in my blatantly revealing costume, toying with the necklace and anxiously waited for Gavin to arrive. I looked pretty damn good thanks to Sophie. We were meeting Austin and Tori at Morris Landing.

The Trail at Morris Landing was like a haunted house outside. They had hayrides, bonfires and costume contests every year. At your own discretion, you wound your way along the trail. Different sections of the trail had its own interactive scene or scenario to haunt you. From the guy chasing you with the chainsaw to the headless woman hanging from a tree, it was like being in your own personal horror film.

I heard Gavin's approach before I saw his car. Fireflies rocketed through me in anticipation. Sophie was coming along for the ride with us, much to Gavin's chagrin. He was like a grizzly bear when things didn't go his way. It was cute.

When the Charger came to a stop, Gavin got out of the car to open my door. He looked good enough to make me wish we could at least drive alone, not that I didn't adore Sophie. I just felt like we really haven't been alone since the night we kissed.

"Hey," I greeted, smiling with happiness. Just the sight of him made me giddy.

"Wow… you look great." His eyes roamed over me in a way that had my entire body reacting. The night air was balmy, but I instantly felt overdressed. And I was practically wearing nothing. Thank God my aunt was still at the shop, I wasn't all too sure she would have let me leave the house tonight, looking like I did.

"Thanks," I replied sheepishly. His gaze was making me subconscious. I had to fight the urge to cover some part of me as I got in the car. Sophie was in the back grinning like a fool.

"I told you," she smugly said before Gavin got back in the car. "This is going to be fun. You do look great by the way."

"So do you." And of course she did. She looked better than great actually. She looked celestial in her angel costume, her long raven hair curling over her shoulders and sprinkled with glitter. She could have just flown down from the heavens. Her eyelashes were decorated with rhinestones, and her sapphire eyes dotted with a tiny star in the middle. "How did you get your eyes like that?" Thinking she must be wearing contacts. I couldn't help but stare at them, trying to see the lenses.

"Magic," she said with twinkling eyes.

I rolled my eyes. Sometimes I swear that I can't get a straight answer from either one of them.

Tori and Austin were waiting for us as we pulled up to the trail, engine roaring. The sign at the entrance threatened in dripping blood. *Don't get left behind, or you might not come back.* As we got out of the car, an ear-splitting scream hit the air. The three of us laughed.

"Looks like the fun as already begun," Gavin said as we walked towards Tori and Austin.

The place was overflowing with the sounds of chatter, spooky music, and creepy chuckles, along with the scent of buttered popcorn and apple cider. Halloween.

"I think I am going to be sick," Tori woefully warned.

"You guys look so cute," I remarked on their costumes.

"Who are you supposed to be?" Gavin asked.

"Janet and Brad from *Rocky Horror Picture Show*," Austin informed. "Tell me you have seen that movie."

"And if I haven't?" Gavin said.

"Oh man, we have got to seriously educate you on films," Austin advised in disbelief.

The five of us paid for our tickets and got in the weaving line. When our turn came to enter the trail, Sophie, Tori and Austin went in first with Gavin and I picking up the rear.

"I think I'm gonna faint," Tori complained. Haunted houses really weren't her thing, but she didn't want to miss out on the fun. Nothing with her ever made sense. She loved to watch the goriest films yet couldn't handle the haunted woods.

The first guy we came across on the trail was decked in rattling chains and covered in gooey fake blood. If I hadn't been preoccupied with walking so close to Gavin, he wouldn't have frightened me. As it was though, I jumped like ten feet in the air and grabbed onto Gavin's arm. Of course he found that hilarious and in my jumpiness, I scared Tori. At this point a fly could scare her, so that wasn't saying much.

"Do I need to hold your hand?" Gavin whispered in my ear, and caused me to shiver for entirely different reasons.

Somewhere along the trail Gavin and I had fallen behind. There was a group in front of us and I think Tori, Austin and Sophie had wound up walking with them. We must have taken a wrong turn because it was all too clear that this tiny path we were following wasn't right. Not to mention there hadn't been a single sign of anyone.

No Freddy Kruger.

No gruesome blood.

No Jack the Ripper.

I don't know how else to explain the fact that I was pretty sure we were screwed.

"This can't be right," I argued. "We're lost," I declared feeling the first inklings of concern. I hoped the entrance sign was prophetic.

"Come on," he said, reaching for my hand. "Let's see if we can find the trail again and get us the hell out of here."

For the next fifteen minutes we walked in what felt like endless circles. A layer of clouds had rolled in above the treetops, and the wind started to pick up. The trees offered little comfort in the blackness.

Pulling out my phone, I glanced at the screen. "Damn it. I have no service," I informed him, deflated. Fingering the stones on the necklace, I nibbled on my lip.

"Something is wrong," Gavin said on guard, shinning the flashlight over the trees surrounding us. "I can feel it."

My anxiety hitched with each step, and the wind whipped against our backs, picking up speed. Dried up leaves covered the ground, crunching underfoot.

Gavin came to stand beside me, scanning the woods. "Bri it's going to be all right," he assured in his steady husky voice.

A twig snapped behind us, and I jerked around expecting the worst.

A faceless horrid monster.

A bloody zombie

A thirsty vampire.

Fear laced through me, while the winds yowled in the distance. "There's something out there." My voice was shaky, and there was no doubt in my mind that we were being watched. Or worse…hunted.

"I promise I won't let anything happen to you." He grabbed my freezing hand. The night had been fairly warm, but with the abrupt change in the wind, it added a bite to the air.

I clung to him, seeking solace. "How are we getting out of here?" My hair blew around in crazy circles, constantly hitting my face. I gave up trying to control the skirt whipping in disarray. The metal coins clattered together in a chaotic musical array.

He must have noticed the chill in my hand. Pulling off his hoodie, he handed it to me. "Here put this on."

"Thanks," I murmured, slipping it over my arms. At once, I was enclosed by his scent. Closing my eyes, I savored the security and warmth instantly. The sleeves fell past my fingertips. When he went to grab for my hand again, he got a handful of cotton. Grinning at each other, I pushed the end far enough for him to get my hand.

"Lucky for you I was a boy scout... more or less."

I gave him a doubtful look but if I trusted anyone to get me out of these confounded woods, it was Gavin. "Let's get out of here," I advised as he led me through a patch of overgrown brush. "Do you think the others are okay?" I asked worrying about Tori, Austin and Sophie.

"They have Sophie. She is better at this stuff than me. They're probably waiting in the car wondering where the hell we are."

I was wondering that as well.

I glanced at my cell phone again, hoping to see a change in the reception bars. Nope. No service at all. It couldn't possibly be that easy.

The only light now was the gleam of blue from the moon. It cast intimidating shadows in all directions, and the little glow from our flashlight. I walked off to the right, looking to see if I could spot anything other than trees. Trees. And more trees.

Then out of nowhere, a deafening sound reverberated through the woods. It was followed by the rapid smacking of branches.

"Bri!" he screamed running straight at me. His eyes were pumped with fear, and my heart accelerated in triple time.

I knew I was in trouble, but the threat hadn't hit me yet. Literally.

Glancing up might have been the biggest mistake. The blood in my veins turned blue, and my legs were paralyzed. Above me was an enormous tree, diving straight at me and knocking away everything in its path. It was only a matter of seconds before it hit, trapping me under its dominant trunk. A scream tore from my lungs, ripping through the forest. The back of my throat burned from the power.

I don't know how he managed to get to me as fast as he did, but he knocked the scream right from my lips. I landed on the ground with an oomph, and Gavin on top of me. My eyes were squeezed shut, waiting for the monstrous impact of the tree. He was breathing hard above me, winded. His head on my shoulder, and my back was pressed into the pine needle forest floor.

As the seconds went by without the blow I was expecting, I cautiously opened my eyes. Afraid of what I would see. The image above me was unexplainable and gravity defying. A part of me thought I was dreaming.

The tree that had been bent on killing me was suspended in the air above us. Just floating. He must have seen my eyes widen, and the shocked gasp that sprung from my mouth. He stared into my frantic eyes. A gush of rampant and rash wind blew through the forest around us, throwing leaves and debris in a whirlwind. The sapphire of his irises burned with a flaming blue more intense than I've ever seen before.

With a sweep of his hand, the hovering tree disintegrated into thousands and thousands of tiny pieces of confetti. The particles rained down on us, covering our clothes, hair and sprinkling in our eyes. The wind continued to protest in anger, pounding with the beat of my heart.

"Make the wind stop," I demanded, utterly freaked. My mind somehow decided that he could even do that, now that I was certain it was Gavin that stopped the tree from pulverizing me.

He bit his lip as he watched me on some internal struggle. Sighing he said, "I can't until you calm down."

I didn't question his reasoning. Right then I just wanted to go home. I tried to focus on evening my breathing, calming the racing in my chest. Hysterics weren't far off.

He ran a hand over my hair, sending the confetti tumbling to the ground, and then trailed a finger along my jaw line. And just like that awareness began to seep inside my body. He was still on top of me and every contour pressed against mine. Perhaps it was the near-death experience, but mostly I knew it was just him. He studied me, marveled by something I didn't understand.

144

A part of me that was always conscience of him was praying he would kiss me. I bit my lower lip to keep it from trembling and was not all that successful. He sensed the change, and his finger moved to outline my lip. I had the deepest urge to drag his finger inside my mouth and taste him. And probably would have to, but now was not the time.

A wandering twig landed beside us. The winds had died and were nothing more than a gentle breeze. Recovering, Gavin stood to his feet and held out a hand to me. "Thank you… for saving me," I said breathy.

"You will always be safe with me," he vowed.

And I knew that there was no one else in the world that would protect me with such ardor and determination.

CHAPTER 15

THE TRIP OUT OF THE forsaken woods was unmemorable. No joke. I didn't remember much of it or how Gavin was able to get us back. And I didn't ask. I assume he did, whatever he did.

Tori, Austin and Sophie were leaning against Austin's car as we came out of the trees. They were all right and by the looks of it, overwhelmed with worry. I doubt the sight of our mud stain clothing and leaf strewn hair helped our cause.

"What the hell happened to you guys?" Tori blurted out at closer inspection.

Wincing, I didn't even know what to say to that. Keeping quiet seemed like the best solution. Someone else could handle this. I wasn't even sure I could handle this.

"We got a little lost and Bri tripped on a fallen tree." Gavin summarized as much as he could without too many probing questions. Sophie didn't look like she bought anything that spewed from his mouth. "I should really get her home," he added.

"Yeah that sounds like a good idea," Austin agreed keeping his eyes focused on my face. I hadn't the foggiest idea of what he saw when he looked at me.

"Austin, would you mind giving Sophie a ride home? I

need to talk to Bri," Gavin said with a *don't ask* edge to his tone.

Austin looked between the two of us trying to judge what was going on. "Sure, no problem. Are you guys really okay?" he asked again.

I could tell he was really worried about me, and my silence wasn't helping. "Yeah, we're fine," I reassured unconvincingly. My voice sounded like a zombie.

"Gavin," Sophie called as my friends turned to leave. "Are you sure this is a good idea?" She gave him a hard look.

"I don't really have a choice." A look passed between them, and Sophie was content with whatever she saw there. She nodded her head and got in Austin's car.

"Let's go Bri," he commanded and led me to the car.

I mechanically got in and sunk into the black plush leather seat. He turned the heat up, chasing the chill from inside and reminding me that I still had on his hoodie. The ride to my house was awkward and quiet. I didn't know what to say to break the silence. My mind was still having trouble believing and processing everything that had occurred tonight. None of it now seemed real. If it wasn't for the awkwardness, it might be all too easy to convince myself it never happened.

We pulled up my driveway, and the little light was radiating on the porch. My aunt had left it on like she always did. That small action made it all rush back to me in a flood of alarm. A part of me thought that maybe I should be afraid. The unknown of what he was and what he might be capable of doing. I studied his profile and just as quickly shut that down, as I realized that this was Gavin. My body screamed that he would never hurt me no matter what he was. I couldn't feel about him the way I did if that wasn't true. Those thoughts alone validated that I would never turn away from him. No matter what I learned. Sorting through those feelings restored a flow of calm.

He turned the key in the ignition cutting off the engine. The keys jingled, slicing through the dead air and followed by his voice. "I don't know where to start. This is all so much harder than I ever thought possible," he admitted. His hands tightened on the steering wheel as he fought to find a way to tell me.

Biting the inside of my cheek, I had no idea how to comfort him or make it any easier. My eagerness was brimming at the surface. I couldn't take my gaze off his form, but he kept his averted. I waited patiently. It was all I could do.

He broke the silence again. "My family wields magic. And has for generations," he revealed in a voice strained with contained control. He flicked his wrist, and the silver woven ring I'd been wearing on my middle finger was in the palm of his hand.

I'd felt a ripple in the air and narrowed my eyes at the ring in his hand. Turning my hand over, I heaved as understanding started to sink in. "Are you telling me that you're a… witch?" My mind whirled with reluctance, even with everything that I had seen with my own eyes. All of it was impossible to believe.

"Yeah I am," he admitted, keeping his eyes focused on the silver ring.

"What do you mean, you're a witch?" My voice caught on a hitch. Maybe I might have lost something in his words. I still couldn't get myself to accept what he was claiming, but if I really let go of the disbelief, I knew it made sense. And that scared the hell out of me.

"You know what I mean," he rebuked, twirling the hoop at his lip, reminding me that this was hard for him also.

Of course I did. Taking a deep breath, I stared at all the luminous stars dotting the night sky. There was so much out there I'd probably never understand. "Your family aren't the only ones, are they?" It only made sense that if they were witches, others existed as well.

"No, witches are everywhere and have been around for centuries. There is an entire organization," he informed and handed the ring back to me.

Whoa, an organization? What like a cult? I wasn't so sure it was such a great idea to just now compare them to a cult.

I took the ring from his hand, slipped it back on my finger and asked, "How does it work? Your magic?" My gut said there was no denying this absurd possibility. The guy that I was absolutely head-over-heels crazy about, was a witch. There was no time to dissect any feelings I might have about the idea. Not with him so close and able to read my emotions.

He finally looked me in the face, and a sigh of relief escaped. "It's hard to explain. Mostly it's control over energy. Everything around us pulses with a life force. Witches are just more in tuned with those energies." He absently toyed with the leather cuff at his wrist.

"Is that why your eyes glow?" I recalled the unusually fiery glow to them sometimes, like tonight.

He nodded his head. "Yeah, the stronger the spell, the more strength it takes, and the more I give myself into the spell. The magic pulsates from inside me."

"Do you just have to think about it for it to happen? The magic?"

"For experienced witches, yeah it's as easy as breathing to cast a spell. For me it is a little more complex. I have to concentrate on the spell and keep it in line with the energy, whether it is my energy, or someone else's energy or matter."

It all sounded a lot harder than I envisioned. Not just a swoop of the hand or blink of the eye (bewitched totally came to mind).

"Some spells come easier, depending on what kind of witch you are," he continued.

"Wait what... There are different kinds of witches?"

His lips upturned a little at the corners. "Yeah... I would need all night to tell you everything I know. We should probably just stick to the basics for tonight," he suggested.

Point taken. "What kind of witch are you?" I asked. That was basic, right?

He shrugged. "My magic specializes in defense spells."

"Defense spells? Like what you did tonight? Saving me?"

He looked out the windshield again, focused on some hidden shadow I couldn't see. "Yeah." His normally husky voice was harsher. "That never should have happened. I should have been able to stop it before it even came near you," he said painfully berating himself.

I hated hearing it. What he had done was save my life. "Hey," I said, touching his arm and forcing his attention back to me. I tried to ignore the zap that always came. "Are you kidding? What you did was beyond amazing. You are always saving me."

"That may be, but that was too close. I should have been more aware of what was going on," he scolded himself.

"I am fine, okay?"

He nodded his head in what I hoped was acceptance, yet his eyes betrayed him. He found himself solely responsible, making me grind my teeth in frustration. My heart thumped at his protectiveness.

There was one more question I had to ask, just to make sure. "What about vampires and werewolves? Do they exist as well?"

He laughed under his breath, chasing some of guilt from his eyes. It was music to my ears. "No... not that I know of." His stance was more relaxed now that I hadn't bolted from the car, and he wasn't down on himself.

"That's a relief." I reached my hand up to feel for the necklace I'd been fiddling with all night, and my hands came up empty. Opening the front of the hoodie, I glance to see if it had gotten under it. Nothing. Closing my eyes, I dropped my head against the back of the seat. "It's gone," I groaned.

"What's gone?" he asked brows drawn together.

"My necklace, the one I was wearing tonight," I hastily replied.

"The one with the moonstone and amethyst? Are you

sure it's gone?"

I nodded my head. "I must have dropped in the woods." There was no way I was getting that back.

"I'll go back and look for it, don't worry about it. I'll find it," he vowed. I could see the determination in his eyes. Everything about this guy was so intense.

I shook my head. "I don't want you going back there. It's fine. I'm sure I could try to replace it." I don't think that I convinced him, but I didn't want him going back there alone.

Yawning, I figured it was well past time I went inside. "Text me tomorrow," I said as I reached for the door handle.

On a whim, I leaned in close to Gavin and pressed my lips softly to his. "Thanks again for saving me," I whispered against his mouth. His head rested against the seat and I'd be lying if I didn't say how much I wanted more. His eyes were still closed as I got out of the car.

CHAPTER 16

WALKING INTO MY ROOM, I half expected some monumental change, proof that life as I knew it wasn't the same. Instead everything was just how I'd left it. My shoe rack still hung over the door, the bed was messy but made, and clothes were still scattered haphazardly everywhere. Quickly tearing off the muddy, torn gypsy costume, I tossed it on the floor with the others. Cracking my window, I let the night air breeze in. Pulling on a tank, cotton shorts and Gavin's familiar hoodie, I breathed in his signature scent, and the floral of my room.

I threw myself on top of my cluttered bed and buried under the covers as the nights events rolled through my brain, like a film. The weight of everything came crashing down like a meteor. Before I could stop, there were unexplained tears streaming down my cheeks. A patter of raindrops pelted the window glass in a sad harmony.

Gavin had saved my life, and the price for it was that I now knew he was a witch. The innocence of the unknown was long gone. I would have to deal with the wonders of the world that I was far from ready to handle. Then there was the fact Sophie was a witch. We had gotten so close. She was the like the sister I didn't have and a good friend. It occurred to me that

I suddenly had as many friends as I did friends with magic, which wasn't saying a whole lot. I had few friends to begin with. Way to balance the scales.

And where in all of this did I fit?

The gentle rainfall mixed with my salty tears and uncontrollable emotions. It sung me to sleep.

Lukas's distant voice penetrated my slumber. He was calling my name, calling me to him. Sometimes it would fade out, nothing but a hush. Then it would grow, beckoning me. I felt like his voice was playing tug of war, pulling me from one side to the other.

He caught me in his arms as I tumbled into the dream. I didn't have to look up to know it was Lukas. He was as familiar to me here as Gavin was in the real world. Or what I thought was the real world. I wasn't sure of anything anymore.

He held me at arm's length, studying my face. After everything, it felt really good to be held. Being in his arms, even briefly, felt like being encompassed in the suns solar. I had to fight back the tears that threatened to consume me again. The emotional outlet left me drained and exhausted. Even here.

"Okay what's going on?" he asked at the sight of my lost and puffy eyes.

You think I would have enough sense in a dream to make myself look hot. Not like I cried myself to bed with useless tears. It was absurd that Lukas looked like a golden angel, and I looked like a train wreck.

"You have no idea," I muttered.

"Tell me," he encouraged.

"Where do I start? How about this? I was almost killed tonight by a tree that came out of nowhere only to be saved by that new guy you are so fond of," I began to ramble out of control, pacing in circles. "And then of course he can't be like any other guy. No. He's a witch –"

"The new guy is a witch," he interrupted not altogether happy.

"Yeah that's what I just said." I was waving an agitated arm in the air.

He ran a hand through his sandy hair. "Unbelievable," he muttered.

"I know right." Yes, someone to share my disbelief.

"Brianna, listen to me. You must be careful. Witches are unpredictable and treacherous," he warned.

He was telling me to be careful? Lukas was a figment of my imagination. And here I thought I had an ally in my astonishment of witches roaming the world. Guess not.

"He could be dangerous," he insisted when I didn't respond and just stood there glaring at him.

What did he know of danger? I couldn't help it. I

snorted, which was definitely a mistake. Gavin had done nothing but protect me from trouble. I doubted it would have made a difference to Lukas. Narrowing his eyes at me, he knew that I wasn't taking him seriously. The annoyance rippled through him and sent a wave of caution in the back of my mind. He had decided to hate Gavin from the get-go. Nothing I could say would change that, his opinion was set in stone. It was written in his stance. However, the need to defend Gavin was overpowering and difficult to disregard.

I shouldn't have brought it up, and I instantly regretted the choice. *What had I been thinking?* That Lukas was a friend, and I could confide in him. I couldn't trust anything anymore.

"Brianna, I am serious," he said offended with clenched teeth. The veins in his neck even started to pulse in annoyance. I've never seen Lukas get upset. Prior to today, I wasn't even sure he had a temper. I guess now I knew. The darkening of his green eyes happened so fast, that I was taken aback.

"I know you are. I'm sorry. It's just that I can't see Gavin hurting anyone," I said defensively.

"Look there is a lot you don't know." His voice was stern with an underlying of impatience.

And apparently he did. Now that I thought about it, he wasn't the least bit surprised when I told him Gavin was a witch. "What do you know about witches…other than they are dangerous?"

He sighed and sat down on the floor of sand. And for the first time I looked around. We were on a small island surrounding by nothing but the midnight waters, exotic flowers and palms. The moon's reflection showed like a globe over the rippling waves. His voice interjected my inspection of the island.

"More than you know. They aren't all dangerous. There are good and evil just like in the human race. Not all witches use their gift with respect and understanding. Many abuse the privileges they were blessed with or get caught up in the power."

Okay that all made sense. Good and evil always existed. I kind of expected that. What I didn't except is for Lukas to know so much about it.

He must have seen the emotions flickering in my eyes. "Brianna I'm not trying to hurt you, just the opposite. I'm trying to look out for you," he argued.

I sunk into the sand next to him. "I just don't know about anything anymore. I feel like I've lost my grip on reality," I admitted, sifting grains of sand through my fingers.

"You haven't," he assured, bumping his shoulder with mine. "This is just beginning."

Crap. That's what I was afraid of.

CHAPTER 17

I SAT BEHIND THE COUNTER at *Mystic's*. My aunt was changing the display for the next season in the front window. Organizing a list of stock that threatened to make me cross-eyed, I took a break sipping on some sweet tea. My aunt had her sleeves rolled up as she worked. Kicking back in my stool, I watched her drape a bronze fabric over the sill. She caught me watching her and grinned.

"How was Morris Landing last night? Did you guys have a good time?" she asked.

"It was definitely filled with terror," I said thinking about my near death experience. Eliminating that tidbit sounded like a good idea. The last thing I needed was her worrying about me every time I left the house.

"I don't know how you guys find that trail fun. It still gives me the heebie-jeebies, and I haven't been there in years."

She had me there. That was going to be the last time I stepped into Morris Landing voluntarily.

"Though with Gavin there, I doubt you had much to be frightened of," she commented, smiling at me mischievously.

"You have no idea," I muttered under my breath. Her insinuation hit so close to home.

"You know I haven't seen Tori or Austin in here for a while. How are they?" she asked.

Tori and Austin would occasionally stop into the store when I worked on Saturday's to keep me company and bug the hell out of me all at once. The guilt that we were drifting somehow made me sick and for my aunt to notice, made it worse.

"Umm, they're good. You are never going to guess what the two of them dressed up as last night." My aunt was very fond of them both and found them humorously entertaining.

"I can only imagine," she said as she started to stack some items on the display.

My aunt wasn't the biggest fan of musicals, but I was, so she suffered through them more times than I could count. "Brad and Janet," I told her and aimlessly played with the straw in my sweet tea.

She was shaking her head smirking. "I should have known it was going to be from *Rocky Horror Picture Show*. The three of you watched it every Halloween."

True we had, except this one. Again with the guilt.

I picked back up my inventory list and started reconciling the items, trying to not think about what a horrible friend I was.

160

***

The bell never rang above the door, but it didn't matter. Where he was concerned, I had an internal alarm. I knew he was there the moment he opened the door. His reckless scent fanned my senses and made me slightly dizzy. He wore jeans and a white tee that hugged his chest.

"Did you use magic?" I whispered when he reached me. He smirked. All the answer I needed.

"Are you trying to sneak up on me?" I asked. "You aren't afraid someone will see you?"

"Most people are too preoccupied to notice something so small," he replied, excitement was brewing in his face. He was up to something.

I guess that meant I didn't count as *most people*. "Oh, I forgot. I have your hoodie. If I'd known you were coming I would have brought it in."

"Keep it," he replied grinning. "I brought you something," he said watching me.

I narrowed my gaze.

"Hold out your hand," he prompted.

I laid my hand palm open on the glass counter and looked into his smiling eyes.

"Now close your eyes."

I glared at him.

161

"Close them," he laughed.

Closing my eyes, I waited for whatever surprise he had in store. A cool metal touched my palm, followed by the weight of something more. I didn't need to open my eyes to see what it was. Just like I knew he had stepped into the shop I knew he had found my necklace. Closing my palm around the stones, the smoothness was reassuring.

"You found it," I said grinning and opened my eyes to be swallowed by pools of shimmering sapphire.

"I told you I would," he reminded me.

"And I told you not to…" I scolded. "Thank you. I'm really glad you did."

He took the necklace from my grasp. "Turn around."

Doing as I was told, I lifted the hair off the back of my neck. He unclasped the necklace and settled it around my throat. His fingers grazed the sides, spearing alertness in every tingling nerve. I shuddered involuntarily and silently mourned the loss of contact. Turning back around, I touched the stones at my throat.

"They'll help you sleep," he said, reminding me of the peculiar lady from the shop. It just occurred to me that she could have very well been a witch. I made a mental note to ask Sophie next time I saw her.

"Do they really have properties like that?" I asked

162

curiously. "The lady who sold this to me…said the same thing," I admitted.

He came around the counter, moved the other stool closer to me and sat down. The fireflies started buzzing. "They do. Crystals and stones each have their own function. Some work stronger than others, depending on how well they are received. These two together, the moonstone and amethyst," he paused and fingered the stones at my neck, causing an all new set of thrills to swirl in my belly. "Work harmoniously together. Especially for you. If I had to pick, these are the ones I would have chosen for you," he informed, letting the stones fall back on my throat. Our knees bumped casually.

"Do you have any stones or crystals?" I was utterly caught in the tone of his voice and his words. He might as well have spellbound me; I was so enamored by him.

He pulled two crystals from his pocket. "Mine are black onyx and obsidian. Protection against black magic," he stated seriously, losing a little of the glint in his eyes.

"Is there a lot of that? Black magic?" My thoughts turned to my dream last night. The warning.

"More than I want to admit. I don't want to scare you Bri," he said. "Magic can be wonderful and exuberating, but with everything there is a price. It isn't meant to be misused. And there are plenty of people out there willing to do just that.

Just as there is light in this world, there is dark."

This conversation was beginning to eerily mirror my dream.

"Have you ever done dark magic," I hesitantly asked, afraid just what the answer might be. Lukas had to be wrong. Gavin wouldn't hurt me.

His eyes roamed to the tile floor in the shop, and for just a second I held my breath with the possibility I might be wrong. "No, I've never given myself over to darkness...but I knew some who did." His expression was filled with pain and hurt as he spoke. "And lost them because of it," he finally said with edgy torment.

"I'm so sorry Gavin," I replied, enclosing his hand with mine, offering him comfort. He stared down at our joined hands.

Toying with a ring I wore on my right finger, he twirled the knotted silver band. "I like hearing you say my name," he softly spoke.

Gravitating towards him, I wanted to close the distance between us. It didn't matter that I was working or that anyone could come strolling through the door. The only thing that mattered was him. I was absurdly disappointed when he pulled back, and it showed all over my face. I had to suppress the groan that formed at my lips. What I should have been, was thankful that someone was thinking clearly. Instead I pouted. Why couldn't he lose all of his control, his focus like me? Why was I the only one suffering?

Just as I was about to voice something stupid, my aunt came through the back door. "Hi Gavin, I didn't hear you come in." She smiled at him.

"Funny neither did I," I muttered.

"I should probably let you get back to work," he said as he got up from his seat. "It was nice seeing you again Clara." My aunt had insisted that he call her by her first name. He paused as he got around the glass counter and looked back at me. "You want to hang out after work tonight?" he asked catching me off guard.

"Sure, pick me at my house?" I wanted to go home and freshen up.

Watching him walk out the door, I sighed.

CHAPTER 18

RACING HOME AFTER WORK I quickly jumped in the shower. I had less than an hour before he showed up at my door. My aunt was downstairs catching up on some reading. Washing my hair in my favorite scented shampoo, I made a last minute decision to shave my legs. The nights were still warm, and since I didn't have a clue what we were doing I figured it was best to be prepared for any scenario.

Slathering on some lotion, I went to my closet to find something to wear. His hoodie lay on the back of the chair and made me smile. The scent of him still lingered on the material, teasing me. Turning back to my closet I slipped on a thigh-length simple white dress, deciding to go with something between dressy and casual. Sitting in front of my vanity, I misted my favorite scent and fussed with my hair. Adding a quick layer of mascara, eyeliner and lip gloss, I finished just as the roar of his engine sounded outside my opened window. The fireflies began to prance in my belly. Swiping the wristlet off my dresser, I ran down the stairs. It was a wonder I didn't break my neck.

The doorbell rang before I hit the bottom stair. I heard my aunt's voice as I rounded the corner, slowing my haste. He was standing in the entryway with my aunt looking dark and dashing. I found it hard to believe that out of all the girls at school, he wanted to go out with me.

"You ready?" he asked me.

Nodding my head, I said good-night to my aunt and followed him out to his car.

"Where are we going?" He had started to pull out of the driveway.

The engine thundered as he punched the gas speeding ridiculously away from town. "You'll see," he responded smirking secretly.

I sat back in my seat and waited impatiently for our destination to be known.

The lights of Wilmington lit the night as we approached the riverwalk. A tint of blood orange hit the coastline, spreading shadows over the quaint shops. Trees twinkled with decorated strands of lights along the plaza. This little coastal place was like a slice of history with its canopy vendors, planked walkways, and charming historical buildings.

"I love the riverwalk. How did you hear about this place?" I asked.

"Your aunt told me how much you like coming here."

"It's so pretty at night." I couldn't help but be flattered by his thoughtfulness.

"Are you hungry?" he asked.

"Sure. There is a really great place right on the water," I volunteered. "They have the best chicken scampi."

"Sounds perfect."

The restaurant was situated facing the ocean and back-dropped by the lights of downtown Wilmington. For this time of night the restaurant was filled with plenty of night-goers. We only had to wait a few minutes to be seated at our table. The view of our booth gazed out over the oceanic boardwalk. There was a cozy, warm atmosphere with the laughter and decadent scents.

The waiter took our drink orders, and Gavin fumbled with his fork. "So I've been meaning to ask you…we haven't had a chance to talk. Are you really okay with me being a witch? I haven't scared you off have I?"

Shaking my head I smiled encouraging at him. I didn't think it was possible for him to scare off the insane feelings I had towards him. "Not hardly."

"Good." He returned my smile.

The waiter came back with our drinks, and we gave him our dinner orders, we both ended up getting the chicken scampi. My mouth watered in anticipation, the food here was out of this world.

I took a sip through the straw of my coke. "So I wanted to ask you if there any other witches in Holly Ridge?"

"No not really. Only one or two that I have seen." He appeared a little uncomfortable, and it made me wonder if maybe I knew them.

"Do they go to our school?" I asked.

He shrugged divulging nothing.

"So they do go to our school." He had my attention now. I wracked through my brain trying to figure out who in the world it could be and came up blank. Looking at Gavin across the booth, I realized he wasn't going to give away any details. So frustrating. There was nothing worse than someone teasing you with a secret, and then not sharing the secret.

Sighing, I went back to sipping my soda as our food arrived. The smell of garlic and pasta was enough to take my mind off it and remind my stomach how hungry I was.

After dinner we stepped out into the glittering balmy night.

"Do you want to go down the riverwalk?" Gavin asked, as we were leaving the restaurant.

"I would love to."

Strolling along the boardwalk, the gentle evening breeze teased the ends of my dress. I imagined this was what a perfect date felt like. For all his dark and brooding qualities deep down there was an extremely great guy, nothing about him didn't make me feel safe. Happily content to walk by his side, I was sure I was the luckiest girl in the universe. The other girls at school could keep their homecoming and proms. I had a witch.

Walking to the end of the dock, I leaned up against the railing, inhaling the fresh, crisp ocean mist. Looking out at the still waters I watched the moon's reflection glistening. His elbow brushed up against mine as he came to stand next to me.

"It's so peaceful. I can't imagine not living near the ocean." I've grown up with it practically in my backyard. It would be like not having a park or a playground.

We sat there enjoying the music of the splashing waves, and the company of each other. Lost in the moment, I looked at Gavin when I felt the air shift with a tingling of magic. I don't know how I knew he was using his gift. Something awoke a sense in me and wondered what he was up to.

He stared into my violet eyes. "Your name is written in the stars," he said, pointing to the night sky over the midnight tranquil waters.

Looking in the direction he indicated I expected some cheesy gesture. Yet what I saw was impressive. The sight he created struck a cord in my romantic heart. Millions of twilight stars dotting above, formed the letters of my name.

"Incredible." There was no downplaying the awe in my voice.

With a wave of his hand the twinkling stars scattered. I watched mesmerized as they reshaped into a perfect single stemmed rose.

Laughing I met his eyes. "I guess being a witch has its high points. That was… magical." I didn't have any other words to describe it.

"I wanted to show you the fun part of being a witch. We're not finished yet."

The ocean sky before us broke out into a spectacular firework display worthy of Fourth of July. Colors exploded against the black night, and his hand closed around mine as we watched the booming spectacle.

"What is everyone going to think?"

He shrugged. "That the city put on an impromptu show."

Hanging out with a witch was proving to be pretty memorable.

When the fireworks ended we headed down the riverwalk towards his car. Hand in hand he lead me though the downtown lights. Most of the shops were closed and only a few bars remained open for patrons. Turning down the alley where his car was parked, I couldn't help but grin about the night we'd had. Never in my wildest expectations had I imagined a night like this. I felt I could ride on the emotional high for months.

Lost in blissful happiness I was shocked when I felt Gavin stiffen beside me. Before I realized what had caused him to become alarmed, I heard the extra shoes clanking behind us along with sporadic laughter. Not a pleasing laughter either, it was the kind that made my skin crawl, and my stomach lurch in fear. Taking a quick glance over my shoulders, I saw the three shadowy figures trailing us.

"Keep walking," Gavin whispered in my ear, drawing me closer to him.

Their footsteps echoed throughout the alley and started to pick up speed as they realized we'd made them. I snuck another peek over my shoulder. An instinctual action I couldn't stop. Like in the horror movies Tori, Austin and I were always watching, the girl who got sliced was always checking over her shoulder at her attacker. We would yell at the girl on the screen who never failed to get sliced and diced.

They had covered more ground than I had imagined. If we didn't start running they were going to catch us. I started to pant from fear and trying to keep up with Gavin's long strides.

"Hey waittt upp," one of the guys called out from behind us, slurring his words. "We only wantsss tooo talk."

They had obviously been drinking if their inability to speak was any indicator.

"Stay behind me," Gavin ordered as he pushed me behind his back.

My hand grasped his forearm, and his muscles bunched under my fingers. "Gavin don't," I pleaded when I realized his intent. I got that he was a witch, but three on one were not very good odds. Witch or not, I didn't want him getting hurt.

"Bri. I am serious." His voice was one I'd never heard before. Hard. Unyielding. "Stay out of the way. You got that?" He looked quickly over at me to make sure I got his point. His eyes were pools of blazing blue fire. They radiated with danger, anger and something darker.

I gulped and nodded.

"Hmm what do we have here." The one with light hair said as they stopped in front of us. "Isn't she something."

I shivered at the hunger in his tone, like a starved stray. He hadn't even so much as finished his sentence when he was thrown up against the brick wall by what appeared to be nothing but air and knocked unconscious to the concrete ground. I flinched at the sound of his body cracking from impact.

"What the hell." One of the other two said confused at his unmoving friend. A moment later the two of them charged at Gavin.

A scream ripped from my throat at the anticipation of

them attacking him. The sound bounced off the narrow brick walls. Before either of them had their hands on him, they were withering on the floor gasping for air. Their hands went to their necks, eyes bulging, and fear of death imminent in their eyes. Gavin stood over them, the space surrounding him crackled with power.

I didn't know what to do, but I knew that if I didn't do something he was going to kill them both. I couldn't let their blood be on his hands. Not even to save me.

"Gavin," I said his name. He didn't budge at my voice. Taking a step closer to him, I repeated his name. The two guys were now gurgling as the last few breaths began to leave their body.

Reaching his side, I put my hand on his arm and yelled. "Gavin stop!" The second I touched him I was jolted with a quick shock. Jerking my hand away, he dropped the spell at the same time. His eyes still had the eerie burning glow and were glossy, like he didn't see *me*.

"Gavin it's okay."

Ever so slowly his eyes cleared and focused on my face. From the corner of my eye, all three of the guys were lifeless but I didn't think any of them were dead.

"Let's go," he ordered. Some of the coldness had left his tone. Seizing my arm he started walking us once again to his car. There was no protest from me. Obediently I got into the passenger seat and buckled my seatbelt. This was going to be a bumpy ride if his mood was any warning.

He tore out of the parking lot, peeling his tires, and the car fishtailed before bolting down the street. It wasn't until we were safely speeding down the road that the effects of what had happened hit me like a bulldozer.

One thing was certain, I wasn't going to cry. Not now. Perhaps later when I was alone, but right now I was going to hold it together.

He had both hands gripping the steering wheel. His knuckles white from the pressure. "Are you okay?"

I ran an unsteady hand through my hair. "I'm fine."

"I'm sorry I lost control. I…" He paused and took a deep breath. "I couldn't let them hurt you."

"It's okay." His expression said he didn't believe me. "Really I'm okay. I promise." And it was true. I was going to survive another day, and I was pretty sure those guys weren't dead.

Pulling up to my house, I was never so happy to be home. The perfect date ended as the date from hell. There was an entire side to Gavin that I had never witness before. His darker side. It should have frightened me. It should have sent me packing. It should have concerned me. The only thing it did do was soften my heart.

"Come over tomorrow? I know Sophie would love to see you," he added. He was worried I was going to fall apart.

"Sure." I was pathetic, jumping at any excuse to see him regardless that I had just witnessed the kind of darkness that lived deep inside of him.

Lukas might have been right. Gavin may be capable of evil things when pushed too far. Yet I thought the same could be said for me, thinking of my own anger issues.

None of it stopped my heart from wanting him.

CHAPTER 19

"I DIDN'T THINK YOU WERE ever going to get here," Sophie said the moment I walked in the door. Apparently her patience level was thin, and she was really excited to see me.

I started thinking of her as the sister I had never had, except she was gorgeous. "Sorry, Gavin never told me when. He just said to come anytime."

"He's such an idiot," she said clearly annoyed.

"Is he here?" I asked, worried about him and slightly disappointed he didn't answer the door.

She started down the hall, with me at her heels. "I think he is upstairs. He knows you're here," she informed in her harmonious matter-of-fact voice.

Following the swish of her floral skirt we walked into the expansive kitchen, the sheer sophistication of the room was mindboggling. I wouldn't even know where to begin cooking in here. There were more appliances and gadgets than I knew what to do with; I'd probably end up losing a finger in the process. The kitchen was flourished in beiges, golds and dark blues. Impressive paintings hung on display around the room. I assumed they were all done by Lily, who was standing in the center.

She was at the granite island nibbling on a feast of snacks she created. A spread of salsa, guacamole, some kind of cream cheese dip and a few others I couldn't identify. There was an arrangement of chips. It looked like the *Food Network* in here. I hoped she hadn't done this all for me. Not to mention if she kept cooking like this, I was going to gain an insane amount of weight.

"Hi Brianna." Lily smiled warmly at me. I couldn't help but grin back. "Have something to eat," she offered.

Taking a seat with Sophie next to me I munched away. "Thanks."

"Can I get you something to drink? Sophie?" she asked us.

Setting two cans of soda in front of us, she mixed a bowl filled with what looked like spinach dip. "So Gavin mentioned that he told you about us," Lily said as I was putting a pretzel in my mouth.

Crap. I had completely forgotten. With everything that happened last night it had completely slipped my mind. This was the first time I'd seen his family since he told me their secret. They were witches. Thank goodness that it didn't occur to me earlier or I would have stressed myself crazy. I swallowed the chip. "Umm, he did," I replied feeling a little uncomfortable. I didn't want them to think I'd tell anyone.

"I just want to make sure that you are okay, and to let you know that if you have any questions… any questions at all, you can ask me. Any of us," Lily offered in a soothing motherly tone. "I can't imagine what you are thinking about all this. It has to be an enormous shock. I can't pretend to understand what it would be like, we've always known. I just want you to know that we will be here to help."

Holy cow. I have no idea what I deserved to receive such honest welcoming, it was almost disconcerting. I didn't want to disappoint any of them.

"Why did he tell you?" Sophie asked next to me. She was swinging her feet under the bar chair. "Don't get me wrong, I am so glad he did. I wasn't sure how much longer I could keep it from you. I don't keep secrets very well from my friends," she confessed between sips of her coke.

"Honey you can't keep a secret at all. Remember that Brianna. Sophie is the last person you tell if you want to keep a surprise," Lily said with a joking twinkle.

Sophie rolled her eyes.

How did I tell Gavin's mom that her son exposed himself to save my life? Not once but twice. I don't think there was any easy way to put it. "He used magic to save my life," I warily revealed, waiting for some kind of astonished reaction.

"Ahh my brother the hero," Sophie teased and popped a

tortilla in her mouth

Not exactly the response I was expecting, but so
Sophie. Remembering Halloween night and trying to forget last
night I thought about the look they shared. I asked, "How did
you know he was going to tell me?"

"Magic," she said with vivacity. "Part of my power is
the future. I always knew he was going to tell you, but the
timing was different, and he was upset with himself. I didn't
know what changed. I also knew that you and I were going to
become fast friends."

Whoa that was a more than a little weird. "You can see
the future?" I asked completely dumbstruck by the idea.

"Sort of. It doesn't exactly work that simple."

Nothing ever does.

She continued, "I see images, places or people. They
are never clear and precise. The future is always evolving
based on decisions and circumstances. Nothing is set in stone,
which makes it so hard to decipher. I only get glimpses," she
explained.

All right that sounded far more complex than I realized
magic could be. There was so much I didn't know or
understand. I was beginning to feel afraid that I wouldn't be
able to fit in or belong to this world. Gavin's world. If I
couldn't exist here what hope would I have with him? Like

everything lately, my world revolved around him.

Sophie shook her head. "Stop worrying. You will always be a part of this and magic will be a part of your future."

I stared at her. She had read my mind or gotten inside my head. I remember what Gavin had said about his sister the night we had coffee. I wasn't sure I liked her in my thoughts. Okay it freaked me out. My thoughts didn't feel safe.

"Did you just read my mind?" I accused.

"No, I can't read your mind, but I can see your aura, and you project your feelings very loudly. Auras are my specialty." You could see the passion on her face. She truly enjoyed her powers.

I gave her a, *what are you talking about* look.

"Very loudly," Lily grinned, echoing Sophie's words.

Just great. Even in magic standards I was odd.

"Everyone has an aura that is dependent upon moods and feelings. Some people are more difficult to read than others. This is my realm of magic. Auras. More so than the little glimpses of the future I sometimes get. I think my ability to see the future opens the channel to tap into it. The closer I am to the person, the easier they are to read. Each emotion is identified by a color, sometimes colors can blend if there are conflicting or multiple feelings. Your emotions are such a part of you that you not only show them, you project them. Loudly."

Great. I needed to work on that somehow.

There was movement from the stairs in the other room, and moments later Gavin walked into the kitchen. "Hey Bri," he said and sat down on the other side of me, carefully eyeing me. He plunked a chip from one of the bowls and popped it in his mouth.

His lip ring moved with the movements of his chewing, and I found it extremely sexy. "Hey," I answered smiling. Trying not to stare, which was harder than it sounded. I toyed with the pop tab on my coke can, anything to distract myself. I wanted him to know I was okay, and he didn't have to tiptoe around my emotions.

"Right now your aura just went through the roof," Sophie giggled.

I wanted to bury my head in mortification, and I seriously hoped she was the only one in the family with that ability, or I was in big trouble. They were all grinning at my apparent discomfort.

"Sophie giving you a lesson in auras?" he asked, as he reached in for more chips.

"I'm getting a crash course. What about you, can you see auras?" I asked, praying he would say no.

"Nope, unfortunately that's never been one of my talents. Just Sophie."

Well thank goodness someone was on my side for once. I turned to Lily who was now cutting up pieces of bread. She was the example of what I envisioned a stay-at-home mom to be. "What is your gift?" I asked curiously caught up in the wonder of it.

"I'm so glad you asked. I am healer of sorts. I dabble in herbs, potions and remedies." She was proud of what she could do. You could hear it in her tone, honest respect for such a powerful gift.

"And Jared and John?"

Gavin laughed. "Jared will have to show you. My dad and I share the same, defensive energy."

Now I was intrigued by the fact he wouldn't share Jared's magic. "Where's Jared?" I wondered aloud.

"He's at class," he informed, loving that he was torturing my impatience.

"You are not going to make me wait. Tell me," I demanded, making them all laugh at my intolerance.

Still grinning he replied, "Nah, it's more fun this way."

Fun for whom I wondered. If I had magic right then, I would have turned him into a toad. It was hopeless; I knew a losing battle when I saw one.

We sat around a little longer, snacking and me listening to their stories about magic. All of it sounded so mystical, electrifying, a dream. Who wouldn't think it would be kickass to be a witch?

I left before it got too late. Tonight I promised my aunt I'd cook dinner, and I was meeting up with Tori and Austin tomorrow to hang out.

I couldn't help but think about how much I would miss not seeing Gavin tomorrow. Utterly pathetic. Between classes during the week, after school at my house, him showing up at my work, I felt disappointed that I wasn't going to see him for one whole day. Pitiable, I know.

He walked me out to my car. This was the first time we were alone since last night. "Are you okay?" he asked looking down at his unlaced boots. There was guilt tracing his words. In my eyes he had nothing to feel guilty for.

I took his hand. "I'm fine. You are always saving me. One of these days you're going to get tired of coming to my rescue."

He smirked, looking a little more like the confident Gavin. "I'm not so sure about that."

I grinned back at him. I didn't want any awkwardness or guilt lying between us.

"Are you busy tomorrow?" he asked.

I silently groaned and wished more than anything that I wasn't busy. Relishing in the few moments we had alone together, I stalled. "Unfortunately, it's movie night with Tori and Austin." His face fell slightly, but I was sure it was all in my imagination.

He reached around me to open my door, brushing my body in the process. My belly jumped on contact, and I don't know what came over me. Maybe it was the near death experiences from the last two nights or the fright I had for him possibly getting hurt. Maybe it was because he never let me down, and no matter what might lurk inside of him, he made me feel incredible, like no one else ever had.

I leaned into him before he had a chance to pull away and put my hand on his waist steadying myself. He smelled like dark sin, and I wanted time to cease. I don't know if it was him or me who made the move, but if I had to guess, it was me. His lips melted to mine in a searing kiss that whisked all the way to my toes. Both of his hands went on either side of the car, boxing me erotically in. His hands never touched me but I swear they were everywhere. Our lips rushed over each other. Caught in pleasure like never before, I teased the hoop from his lip with my tongue, loving the coolness against the heat in my mouth and trying to push him further. Toying with his mouth, I tempted him to take the plunge.

His lips broke from mine and trailed down my throat over the pulse that hammered there. "You taste like strawberries," he murmured against my neck causing a shudder to rack through my body. Our lips met again, and I dug my hand into his silky hair. His name tumbled from my lips, and with the moonlight overhead, I gave into him. Where he was concerned, I had no control.

We were so wrapped up in each other that we didn't see the beam of headlights that came out of nowhere and shot across his driveway. We both sprang from each other's arms. Shaken, Gavin ran a hand through his messy hair and jammed both hands in his pockets. Like he was afraid he would reach for me again. I sunk back against the car hugging my arms over my chest.

Jared walked up, dimples grinning. "That was hot," he said as he passed us by to the house.

The moment was broken even while my insides were still humming.

"See you Monday," he said huskily as I got into the car, and he shut the door.

I drove home in a heart pounding daze. It wasn't until I got home that I realized I'd missed my chance to ask Jared what his powers were. My mind had been too muddled with the exotic taste of Gavin.

CHAPTER 20

MOVIE NIGHT WITH MY BEST friends was never without its drama. I felt the need to try and get our friendship back on track. We hardly did any of the things we used to, and it was eating at me. So I was on my way to Tori's where she and Austin were no doubt picking some horrid slasher movie, bent on scaring the crap out of us. We'd been doing this exact thing since we were little.

Tori had a huge theatre room on the first floor of her mansion. It was seriously large. Her Tudor style brick home was on the other side of Holly Ridge, and the driveway was like a mile long with a gated entrance. I let myself in through the double front doors. Her step-mom was probably at some outrageously priced spa, and her dad lived at work.

Their bickering over which movie to watch, echoed down the vast hall. Just like old times. Smiling, I kicked off my shoes and headed down the hallway. The smells hit me the closer I got. Popcorn. Butter. Brownies. They were our signature snacks, creatures of habit. She had one of those old fashion popcorn makers; I could hear the pop-pop-pop noise as I pushed open the door.

The two of them were standing in front of the towering shelf that housed movies of every genre lining the back wall.

187

"Hey guys," I greeted. Tori had the pillar candles lit around the room. Their sweet aroma mixed with the buttery popcorn.

"Good you're just in time," Tori replied, the bangs of her light brown hair hung over her chocolate eyes.

"So what are we watching," I asked plopping into one of the huge leather recliners.

"It's a toss between the new *Saw* or *Final Destination*. Tori's being a diva," Austin proclaimed eyeing her, hand on his hip.

They were always on each other. I think they enjoyed the squabbling, like an old married couple.

"I am seriously not the only diva in this room," she animatedly retorted, pushing the hair from her face.

"All right guys I'll decide." Thinking I could end this before it got out of hand.

"No," they unanimously bellowed.

"*Final Destination* is fine," Tori conceded, pulling out the case.

Just like I thought. Apparently my taste in films sucked. Whatever. As long as we got this movie rolling.

She opened the DVD case and hit about a gazillion buttons before the movie actually started to play. Her TV and Blu-ray equipment frightened me as much as blood and gore.

She hit the light switch as Austin took the recliner next

188

to me. He handed me a bowl of popcorn with a brownie in the middle. I settled in my seat and waited for the credits to role.

"You better not jump in my lap," Austin warned grinning. He looked so cute in his Dolce and Gabbana gear and smelled like expensive cologne.

"Funny, just remember *you* sat next to me. It's not my fault if you lose an arm." I was notorious for jumping out of my seat or grabbing whoever was lucky enough to sit beside me. I couldn't help it, scary movies made me skittish.

"Sometimes you're more fun than the movie," he teased, but I'm sure there was truth to it.

I threw a piece of popcorn at his head and then shoved a handful in my mouth.

"You're going to regret that later," he threatened. It was only a matter of time before he got me back. "Where's dark and sexy tonight? You should have brought him along. He could have been dessert." Austin practically drooled at the prospect, and I was right there with him. I hated to admit it, but I missed him. A ton.

I shrugged. "I don't know. I didn't think about it," I admitted, not completely true. I always thought of him.

"Does he taste as good as he looks?" Austin purred.

"Better," I assured amused, both of us grinning wickedly. I refocused my attention back into the movie, which was difficult now that I'd pictured Gavin.

Halfway through the film I managed to only attack Austin once, and his arm survived. But he started to lean out of my reach. It was around then that I began to get a chill. Not the kind where I was cold, but the creeped out kind. I tried to convince myself that it was just the movie but my body wouldn't listen. My concentration was blown, and I couldn't shake the ghostly feeling that someone was watching me, like those moving eyes in a painting. The images on the projection screen forgotten, I scanned the candle lit room trying to find the source of my discomfort. I even stared hard at the cinema posters hung on the walls. Mentally I made a note to ask Gavin about ghosts. In the mean time I was going to pretend that this paranormal activity was a hoax.

"Austin, knock it off," I whispered, even though I knew it wasn't him.

"What?" he asked, confusion flickering in his eyes.

"Nothing," I grumbled, incapable of shaking the negative vibes that started to crawled over my skin like centipedes. I had the feeling of being trapped on my own horror set. Even scarier, no one else knew it. Now that I knew real evil existed, I was more on edge.

The vibe permeated the air and slithered along the floor, withering between the recliners. There wasn't anything visible to be seen, but I could picture it all the same. My eyes ran over the row of recliners behind us, and I tucked my feet underneath me. No way was that creepy thing tugging on my toes.

"What are you staring at?" Austin whispered watching me.

He rattled me out of my trance. I had to pull my eyes from the floor. "Nothing," I mumbled, not wanting him to think I was off my rocker, a true possibility.

"Are you sure? No offense, but you look pale and your eyes are weird," he stated honestly.

Tori leaned out over her chair. "What is going on?" she demanded of the interruption.

A sweeping wind came barreling across the room. I studied both of their faces waiting for the astonished look. It never came. The movement gave me goose bumps, and the instinct to run. It prickled at the back of my neck. Moments later the room was engulfed in darkness as the flames from the candles extinguished. That got their attention. I heard Tori's gasp and Austin prattled, "What the hell."

"That was bizarre," Tori complained, hitting pause.

An understatement and she took the words from my mouth. Movie night was over for me. I needed to get out of here before I did something completely irrational and stupid, like tell them I feel ghosts or I am being haunted by some supernatural being. Or whatever crazy notion my mind could concoct.

"I'm sorry guys, but I think I should go home. I'm not feeling so well," I admitted, totally true if you considered my mental health.

"You need to get home before your ass faints on us," Austin proclaimed. "You look like you've seen a ghost."

A hysteric laugh escaped my lips.

"Are you sure you can drive?" Tori asked, obviously thinking I might pass out at the wheel or was delusional.

"Yeah, I'll be fine." I got up to grab my things.

I raced down her driveway and slammed myself into my car. Quickly locking the doors, I turned the key and shifted in reverse. The need to escape was wild inside me. I needed distance from whatever *that* was. Shoving my free hand in my purse, I dug around for my phone.

He answered on the second ring, "Are you okay?" Gavin asked, pathetic that those were the first words out of his mouth. Was I really that screwed up?

"Are there ghosts?" I inquired immediately, trying to keep my voice even and not psychotic.

"What are you talking about?"

"I don't know. I mean I do know. It's just…" I started crazily rambling. *Get a hold of yourself.* "I was wondering if there are ghosts here… with us?"

He was silent on the other end, not a good sign. "Yeah there are some spirits that walk this plane. Where are you? I'm coming to get you," he demanded.

"I'm driving, I just left Tori's and am almost home," I told him. Actually I had just passed his street.

"I'm on my way over." He hung-up, never even waited for me to respond.

The dial tone rang in my ear. I looked at my clock. It was late and most likely my aunt would be sleeping. I never snuck a boy into my house before; there was a first time for everything. "Great," I said to no one in particular. Hitting the gas, I raced to make sure I beat speed demon to my front door. I prayed that he didn't wake up the entire neighborhood with the sonic boom engine of his.

Pulling up my driveway, I turned off my lights, grabbed my bag from the passenger seat, and opened my door. Rummaging for my house key, I turned toward the house and bumped into something solid.

"Shit!" I yelped, looking up into to Gavin's shadowy face. "You scared the hell out of me," I accused, hitting him on the arm.

He put a finger to his mouth and hushed me. "Shhh, you are going to wake up the whole block."

"Me," I said. Glancing at the rear of my car, I saw there was a little white Jetta parked behind it. "That's not your car."

He raised the eyebrow with the silver bar. "I know. I borrowed my moms. My car would wake the dead, and I figured that wasn't such a good idea this late."

He was killing me here. I ran a hand through my hair and leaned back against my car. "How did you get here so fast?" He didn't live far, but I literally just pulled in.

"Have you seen me drive? Though the Jetta doesn't have the greatest pick-up."

I rolled my eyes. "Whatever. Let's get inside." I was still freaked out but I knew I was safe now.

Cracking the front door, I peered inside checking to make sure my aunt was indeed sleeping. The coast looked clear. All the lights were turned off except for a small one in the kitchen. Motioning with my head, we slowly walked through the kitchen and up the stairs to my room.

I closed the door to my bedroom carefully behind us and turned the lock with a tiny click. He'd been in my room before, but never like this.

The clothes I had on from tonight smelled like popcorn and probably had buttery stains smeared on them. "I need to get out to these clothes real quick. I'll be right back," I whispered.

He grinned devilishly at me, and I knew that this was going to be a long night.

There was a small bathroom connected to my room, rushing I changed into the first thing I found, a tank and shorts. The moonstone and amethyst necklace sat at my throat. I ran a comb over my hair, brushed my teeth and applied some strawberry lip gloss.

He was sitting on my bed when I finished, looking sinful. I stood at the door a moment feeling nervous, jittery, and energized all at once. He watched me with his eyes as I walked across the room and sat cross legged on the bed next to him.

"Tell me what happened," he asked keeping his voice low.

The room was dimly lit by my ornate desk lamp. "I don't know. It's probably nothing."

"If it was nothing you wouldn't be upset and you wouldn't have called me," he rationed.

He was right. I sighed. "I was at Tori's and we were watching a movie in her theatre room. I started to feel this... presence like we weren't alone. It's hard to describe," I said biting my lip. "I couldn't see anything, but I knew it was there. Does that make sense?" I asked uncertain.

He nodded his head. "Yeah, it makes perfect sense. You

are a magnet for trouble."

I grabbed the nearest thing I could find and chucked it at his head. He caught the pillow in midair and grinned at me.

Ignoring him, I continued, "And then I started thinking about ghosts. Tori had a lit a bunch of candles earlier, and they all went out at the same time. It was so strange." What I didn't say was how *bad* whatever *it* had felt.

"I leave you for one night and you start hanging out with the wrong crowd," he joked. Though under the teasing tone was caution. "I'm sure it was a spirit. What I don't know is if it was seeking you or something in Tori's house."

I glanced down at my hands twining the bedding. "It – it felt personal," I grudgingly admitted.

"That's what I'm worried about." There was a line of apprehension on his brow.

"I don't understand," I said frustrated. Lying down on my pillow, I groaned.

He laid down next to me, our faces no more than a breath away. Staring at the ceiling he swirled his hand in the air. "Let's worry about it later."

Sighing, I glanced above and watched as sparkling shooting stars beamed across my ceiling. Their tails left stardust trailing behind them and it scattered over our heads. He knew just how to distract me.

"Don't leave," I said softly. The idea was wild and reckless, but I couldn't let him go. For reasons beyond my control I needed him. My safety depended on it. My sanity depended on it. My heart depended on it

He twined our fingers together. "I won't leave you Bri," he promised.

He opened up his other arm, and I moved into his embrace. Laying my head on his chest, I listened to the even, rapid beat of his heart. His free hand played with the strands of my hair, sending a different kind of shooting stars down each tendril. There was nothing in my world that even came close to the experience of being in Gavin's arms. I doubted there ever would be.

CHAPTER 21

I CORNERED HIM FIRST THING in the morning at school. "Hey, what happened? You were gone when I got up this morning," I loudly announced irritated. I knew I was looking for a fight when I woke this morning alone, and God dammit he wasn't going to disappointment me.

He shut the door to his Charger. "Calm down Bri," he advised in an even controlled tone, so unlike anything I was feeling right now.

The sky had been sunless and gray when I'd left my house. Clenching my teeth together, the surge of anger rushed me. "Don't tell me to calm down." Each word layered the streaming heat pumping in my vessels. It was slipping out of my control again, and there was nothing I could do about it.

People began to take notice of us in the parking lot, but they were the least of my concerns.

"Okay. I won't," he answered to composed for my liking.

"Don't patronize me," I hissed, teeth still ground together. The sky darkened and clouds rolled in turmoil above.

A small crowd had stopped and glanced our way. "I think we should go somewhere else to finish this," he advised lowering his voice.

Throwing my arms in the air the winds started to howl. "I don't care about them," I barked.

He took a deep breath, trying to figure out how to best handle me. "Look Bri, I had a good reason. I was looking out for you."

"How was that looking out for me?" I yelled at the same time the sky opened up and crackled with lightning and exploded with thunder. The oncoming storm fed the anger I was feeling, feeding it with its electrifying currents.

His eyes looked up at the violent show above and took a step towards me. "I thought it would be best if I was gone before your aunt found us," he explained, his voice stable.

The mention of my aunt weakened a chip in the wall of fury I'd been building. In the rational part of my mind I knew he totally had a point. But that still didn't absorb the illogical disappointment turned insane rage I felt at waking without him. I was treading on dangerous ground and becoming irrationally dependent on him. The one night with him had spoiled the rest of my nights forever. His scent still lingered on my sheets and would taunt me for nights to come I was sure.

"You said you wouldn't leave," I argued, the root of my hurt.

His arm reached out tentatively for my hand.

Lightning lit crazy patterns in the sky. "Don't touch me!" I yelled and stepped out of his reach. The haze had not yet entirely receded. I was afraid I would hurt him. And hurting him would kill me.

"I'm sorry Bri," he professed.

The last bell for first period rang, and the parking lot was mostly empty now except for a few stragglers who were hurriedly trying to seek shelter.

Tears started to burn my eyes, spilling over my flushed cheeks. They were washed away by huge raindrops that began to pour from the ominous clouds. Wiping away the tears and rain with the back of my sleeve, I shook my head unable to speak. I was feeling ashamed of this out of control violence in me, ashamed that I was crying, and most of all scared that I loved him. I turned and walked away.

"Bri," he called, and I knew it was only seconds before he caught up with me. I wasn't really prepared to go up against a witch, but I had to get away from him. Taking off at a full run, the rainfall pelted me in the face. My own tears drenched and blurred my eyes.

Defying the elements and any reasonable explanation, I made it to my car and fumbled with the lock.

"Bri," my name sounded behind.

Slamming the door shut, I revved the engine and pealed

out of the parking lot. My eyes were glued to his as I approached him. They were glowing with magic. I knew that there was only a very slim window of opportunity to escape what he was brewing, but I had to try. Pressing down hard on the gas, I floored the poor aging mustang. *Please let me through, please let me through*, I repeated over and over again. Once I reached the main road, I eased up on the gas and took a much needed breath. I hadn't the foggiest idea what just happened, but I wasn't going to look a gift horse in the mouth.

Now that I had ditched school again just where the hell did I plan on going? There was only one place I really wanted to be right now. I thought it was a pretty good idea to hurry. There wasn't much time before Gavin would be following me in his much faster Charger. This car had no hopes of out running that, not in its present condition, and there was no doubt in my mind that he would be at my wheels.

Every few minutes I would check in my rearview mirror expecting to see his black muscle car trailing me. My face was salt streaked from my dried up tears, and the storm looked to be passing on, but still left the sky darkened from the aftermath. It wasn't until I pulled up to a secluded section of Topsail Beach that I relaxed.

Getting out of the car, I was hit with my favorite smells and sounds. The crisp, clean ocean air, and the gentle lulling waves, the sound itself was enough to bring me peace. Walking down the wood planked boardwalk, I was glad to see few people wandered the beach. If there was anything I wanted right now, it was solitude. Pesky seagulls dive bombed the churning waters in an attempt for a fresh catch.

Finding a spot just far enough from the shoreline to not get wet, I sat down hugging my knees to my chest. I lost myself in the rippling of tides washing over the sand, uncovering seashells from the depths of the ocean floor. As a little girl, my aunt took me here every week in the summer. We spent hours gathering shells, playing in the unpredictable waters, and making up stories about the mermaids who lived below those rapid waves. I always had a fascination with mermaids as a kid, thanks to Ariel.

Right then that memory made me miss my aunt in a way that I hadn't in a long time. An ache bloomed in my chest. No longer wanting the solitude I original sought, I wished she was here. Closing my eyes I laid my chin on my knees, basking in the sounds. I don't know how much time past when I felt him.

"How did you find me?" I asked before he made his presence known.

He sat down beside me in the sand, his shoulder touching mine. "Magic."

I hadn't thought about him being able to track me. The idea was both disconcerting and relieving. He'd always be able to locate me. "I bet you're no fun to play hide and seek with," I said. My heart swelled that he cared enough to look for me.

His lips upturned at the corners. "Sophie never thought so," he replied.

"It isn't something Sophie can do?" I wondered aloud, more than willing to avoid what had driven me here in the first place.

"No and it drives her nuts."

"How does it work?" I asked.

He shrugged. "It's part of a defense spell. Easier when it is someone I care about," he explained.

I swallowed thickly.

"It's a locating spell. The closer I am to the person the faster I can locate them, but I can find anyone if I have something personal of theirs. Though that spell takes time," he finished.

That had me thinking. "How long have you been here?" I asked holding my breath, waiting in anticipation.

His sapphire eyes held mine. "I watched you walk down the boardwalk. I needed to make sure you were safe," he defended.

I exhaled and warmth spread in my chest. He'd been

able to find me within minutes or even seconds. He cared for me, but I wanted more than friendship.

"You got a spell for ditching school?" I teased.

"Don't worry I took care of it," Gavin assured me, which I assumed he did some kind spell to excuse me from school for the day. Regardless, I was grateful.

I looked out over the vast ocean. "I'm sorry about earlier. I don't know what I was thinking. You did the right thing by leaving," I admitted. "It's for the best that my aunt didn't find out." It never even occurred to me that his family might have been wondering where he was all night. I hope that I hadn't gotten him into any trouble.

"We need to talk. There's something that I think you need know," he stated serious, surprising me. I knew that this wasn't just a friendly chat. What other secrets could he possibly have bigger than wielding magic? My mind spun trying to figure out what this was about. The events of today seemed to somehow have triggered this *talk*. And that frightened me.

"Okay," I said tentatively, not really sure what was going on or what to expect.

"Since we have the day off… What do you say we go to my house?" he suggested grinning.

"Your parents won't care?" I asked thinking that his

mom was usually home painting.

"Nah but Sophie is going to be pissed when she finds out that I did this without her."

I gave him a blank look.

CHAPTER 22

I FOLLOWED HIM IN MY car to his house.
Thankfully he kept it to a reasonable speed for my slow
chugging mustang. By the time we arrived my stomach had
wound itself into a thousand pretzel knots.

"Gavin?" his mom questioned when we walked in the
house. She didn't appear as angry or upset as I pictured. If
anything she looked startled and baffled. She had a brush in
hand and paint splattered on her hands and apron. I envisioned
this situation if it was reversed, and we had walked into my
house. My aunt would already be taking my head off about not
being at school. The Mason's definitely had a different policy
about attendance than my family.

"Bri and I had an altercation at school this morning,"
He began.

That was an understatement. I shifted my feet feeling
uncomfortable.

"Which led to a little bit of unexplainable magic, I
covered my tracks but I thought it would be best if I had that
talk with Bri now," he explained like it was the most natural
thing in the world.

The mention of our fight this morning caused my
cheeks to bloom red. I wasn't proud of what happened and had

hoped we'd keep it between us. Guess not.

"Hmm I see. I wondered when you would get to this," she stated, wiping her paint stained hands on the front of her apron.

The fact that she knew what was going on and I was clueless unnerved me to say the least. I felt like I was walking blind into a busy highway.

"I don't have much choice. She needs to know," he said.

"She does," Lily agreed and looked over at me. "Brianna, remember that if you need anyone to talk to I am a great listener."

I nodded my head confused more than ever and followed Gavin to the backyard of his house. The yard was fenced beautifully with decorative framing and offered privacy between the house and the beach. I could hear the water spraying over the rocky shores, infusing the air with salty surf.

He turned around and faced me. Biting the bottom of his lip, his sapphire eyes searched mine. "When I first met you I recognized something of myself in you. It's what drew me to you. I spent the first few weeks waiting for you to acknowledge it. And when you didn't, it puzzled me. I thought maybe you were playing a game. I couldn't figure you out. It was my mom who brought it to my attention that you didn't know. And I thought how does she not know? Truthfully I still don't know how it came to be that you weren't told, but if I had to guess it has something to do with losing both your parents." He ran a hand through his dark hair and exhaled. "I want to show you something first. Give me your hands," he instructed.

I eyed him with hesitancy and interest, my heart thumping wildly in my ears. Nothing he said made sense and was probably written on my face. Regardless, if there was anything I knew about Gavin it was that I trusted him. Placing both of my hands on top of his, palms up, I tried to ignore the spark that ignited at contact.

Keeping his eyes locked on mine he said, "Relax."

Easier said than done, my brain was on overdrive. Taking a deep breath I inhaled the moist air and tried to calm my anxiety. The feel of his hands under mine was encouraging.

"I want you to think about the warmth and glow of a light, any kind of light. Envision it inside your head," he advised in his husky voice, making it difficult to concentrate on anything else.

Not questioning what he said, I just did what he asked. I thought about the yellow shining of starlight. How the beams surround the star, lighting up the sky, how each gave off their own natural light. I linked their burning glow to that of a flame, intense heat.

"Now keep that image. Think inside your head *Luminescence*. Repeat it."

My gaze was locked on to his, and I felt sort of detached from the rest of my body. An underlining hum buzzed along my arms, traveling through my veins like when you get an IV. I could feel it mixing with the heat of my blood, like an elixir.

Luminescence. Luminescence. I repeated, my eyes never wavering from his, my body singing with an intoxicating high, the taste of something pivotal on the tip of my tongue.

Like a gust of flames my hands erupted with a soft glow of dazzling light. A gasp slipped from my mouth as I watched the light prance over my hands, mesmerized. The flames didn't burn like a natural fire but tickled. My hands tingled where I could feel the magic fluttering. It was like nothing I've ever felt before

Illuminating.

Invigorating.

Freeing.

Looking through the luster I smiled at Gavin watching my reaction. "It's beautiful," I said.

"This is one of the most basic spells. To make light," he explained. "Can you feel the energy feeding the magic?" He asked.

I didn't know exactly what I was looking for. I mean there was that zing I got when we touched, but more prominent now was a buzzing pulse. "Yeah I think I can feel it," I admitted.

We grinned at each other. What he could do was breathtaking, and I admired his gift. "This is amazing," I told him.

Taking a step back, he moved slowly away. "Don't move. Just stay where you are," he advised. He carefully removed his hands from underneath mine as he backed away.

"You can share magic?" I asked confused when he dropped his hands to his side.

He shook his head. "No, I can't. This –" he indicated with his arms. "Is all you."

"What – t," I stammered, eyes wide. The light in my hands flickered.

"It's your magic," he said softly.

Shaking my head in denial at his words, "That can't be. I don't have magic," I refused. The glow dropped from my palms, and the humming with it.

"You're wrong," he stated. "I've been aware of the power in you the second we met. What took me awhile to understand was that you didn't know. It stumped me that you didn't recognize what I was."

I was still shaking my head in denial. Refusing to believe anything he said. "What are you saying?" my voice bordering frantic.

"You know what I'm saying, and you know I'm right. Witches can always identify another witch, the energy they wield."

"Why are you doing this?" I asked trying to keep the disbelief and anguish from my voice.

"Because it's the truth. I thought it would be easier to show you," he reasoned.

"Easier!" I shrieked.

"I'm trying to help you Bri."

I believed that he thought he was. It hurt nonetheless. "I'm not a witch," I argued.

He looked exasperated with my stubborn refusal that he so honestly believed. "You used magic earlier today to get out of the school parking lot. I was shocked that you were able to overpower my spell without really knowing that you could. And that is not all," he added when he saw that his argument wasn't breaking through. "Have you ever noticed how the weather can mirror your moods? You can weathercast. I saw it the day we met, Halloween night when you were scared and today, the storm. Indirectly you've been using your magic."

Everything he said sort of made sense, however I didn't

think it was proof that I was a witch. How much of it could be considered coincidence? He might have started to put doubt in my mind but I wasn't admitting to anything.

He saw the uncertainty begin to ease its way into my eyes. "You are not only a witch, but there is something different with your energy, something unique, extra. I've been trying to pinpoint it. I just don't know what it is."

Freaking great. Was that supposed to make me feel better? Not only was I supposed to be a witch, I was some super mutant witch on steroids.

"I know you think I'm a witch, but I'm not," I retorted even though I was beginning to discredit everything I thought I was or knew about myself, it began to wiggle its way in. The anger that got out of control, the welts I'd left on Rianne's arm and a gazillion other little things I was beginning to remember that I'd always brushed off. How could I be a witch and not know?

"I'm not the only one," he stated. "My whole family knows you're a witch. I told you that we can recognize one another."

I had forgotten about Lily, Sophie and the rest of his family. My whole world felt like it had just tumbled down on top of me like a nuclear bomb, the damage irreparable.

"Look, I know this is a lot to take in, but I want you to

know that I am here for you, and I want to help," he said closing the space between us.

I took a step in retreat and watched as his eyes flickered. The only thing I wanted right then was to get out the hell out of there. I didn't want to be bombarded with questions, sympathy looks or even admit what they all believed. The Mason's might be ready to call me a witch, but I was far from ready or eager.

"I've got to go," I said and turned walking towards the gate.

Away from the one guy I thought got me. Away from a family I admired. Away from the possible truth.

I looked over at him, before I opened the iron door. "And don't follow me... please," I pleaded.

His eyes fell, causing an ache in my chest. It didn't stop me from walking out the door and getting into my car.

CHAPTER 23

ONCE I REACHED THE PROTECTIVE barrier of my car, I laid my head on the steering wheel and gave up trying to sort all the scrambling thoughts. By the time I managed to pull up my driveway I felt like the walking dead. My entire body was numb and detached from my brain. I couldn't feel anything. Letting myself into the house, I tossed my keys on the entry table and zombie-walked to my room. Shutting the door behind me, I climbed into bed fully clothed and wrapped the covers around me. My eyes affixed on the ceiling above. Each time I closed them I saw myself in different forms, all of them depicted me as a witch.

In a black dress whipping around me in violence, me in another variation of the same dress in red standing at the edge of cliff with my hands thrown in the air. No matter what I did, it was always the same and always with an underlying of evil. It got to the point where I didn't close my eyes anymore. I laid there clutching the moonstone and amethyst necklace. Praying it would chase away the visions.

Sometime later that night my phone vibrated on the nightstand. Ignoring everything around me, I continued to stare at the ceiling, falling in and out of reality. There was no concept of time. No sense of the room around me. No desire to move. Just the numbness I came to depend on, to shut out the truth. When my aunt came home and opened my door to check on me, she assumed I was sick. In a way I was. The bowl of chicken noodle soup she fixed me before going to bed, still sat on the nightstand beside the bed untouched and cold.

By morning I laid in the same position, in the same trance-like emotionless state. Before my aunt left to open the shop she knocked on my door.

"Brianna?" she called cracking the door and peering inside. All the lights were off and the blinds closed, darkness consuming me. I was still tucked in bed. My eyes were opened, looking nowhere in particular. She came and sat on the edge of my bed beside me. Pushing the hair back from my face, she eyed me warily. Her floral perfume hit the room and soaked into my soul, breaking it a little. I was afraid she was about to open the floodgates I'd been numbly holding back.

"Hey honey, still not feeling good?" she asked.

"No not really," I managed for her sake. I wasn't in the mood for conversation as my throat started closing up with overwhelming emotion.

"Okay, I'll call the school and check on you later. If you need anything, call me at the shop." She picked up the uneaten soup bowl as she left and paused at the door. "You should really try and eat something," she advised concern touching her voice.

The tears poured as the garaged door shut. Huge, sob-racking tears tore from deep inside me. The kind that gave me hiccups in an effort to breathe and cry at once. I curled the blanket around me and hugged myself in a ball. The windowpanes in my room pounded with giant raindrops which made me cry all the more. A justification of my uncontrollable magic I didn't want. My blanket was soaked with my sobbing, and my chest heaved irrepressibly. The crying jag was long overdue. Locking away my feelings was never good for me or apparently the weather either. Now with the knowledge that I could somehow cause storms, I didn't know what to do.

I knew the moment school started, the vibrating of my phone filled the room. Turning over I drowned out the noise. And so my day went. My body felt achy and weak when I finally tore myself from bed. It never occurred to me before how lost and alone a person could feel. I'd never been so unsure of anything in my life. There were two options here. I either accepted that I was a witch like Gavin claimed, or I went on and resumed my life being blissfully ignorant. Neither sounded like a viable solution.

Downstairs I nibbled on some crackers, trying to settle my empty stomach. I thought about the results of ignoring the possibility I was a witch. I could potentially harm others by not being able to control my magic. I could disappoint those who cared for me. Most of all I could lose Gavin. It all boiled down to being scared. Scared to be a witch. Scared at failing. Scared to lose the guy I was probably in love with. Scared to lose my friends and potentially my aunt. I wasn't sure I could risk all that.

I spent the remaining part of the day going over and over the same questions with no answers. When night fell I was in bed again before my aunt got home. Much like the previous night she came in to check on me. This time I forced myself to eat a little of the soup she brought and wished that I could open up to her about what was eating at me inside.

Laying the necklace on the nightstand after my aunt left, I knew of only one person to whom I could talk. Whose opinion wouldn't matter. After all, he was a figment of my imagination. And true to the properties of the necklace I wore lately, I hadn't had a single dream of him.

Lukas. I thought his name as I drifted off to sleep. My eyes fluttered as I slowly went under. His name whispered from my lips.

As I opened my eyes, and the first thing I saw was the lilac frost of my bedroom walls. *Hell*, I thought it didn't work. Frustrated I tossed the covers aside and turned on my bedside

217

lamp. Tousling my unwashed hair, I made a mental note to shower tomorrow. Just because my life was falling apart didn't mean my hair had to suffer.

I sat up in the bed and yelped at the figure sitting at my desk chair. His grin was one I knew well.

Lukas.

"Holy crap you scared me to death," I cried.

"You look like hell," he replied grinning from ear-to-ear. He ducked from the pillow I tossed at his head and laughed.

Rolling my eyes I asked, "What are you doing here?" Here as in my bedroom.

"What do you mean, you brought me here like always," he answered looking at me like I lost my mind. Maybe I had.

"I'm dreaming?" This was a first. I've never dreamed of my own life, nothing this personal and certainly not my bedroom. And again why does my subconscious continue to make me look like I just rolled out of bed. If I was a witch, at least I should be able to spell myself hot.

"Pretty sure," he commented. "Nice room." His smile was infectious. "I always wondered what it would look like."

He got up from his seat, the college t-shirt he wore spanned his chest and strolled around the room, looking at the most intimate part of my life. There was a slight sting in my chest at having another guy in my room, even if it was in a dream. He came across the necklace on the table beside me.

"So this is why I haven't seen you lately," he said, trailing a finger over the moonstone and amethyst gems.

"How do you know that?" I wondered aloud.

He shrugged and sat down on the bed next to me. The mattress shifted under his weight, and his blue jeans rubbed against my bare leg. "My mom taught me," he replied.

We never really talked about his parents before, and it made me wonder about them. I always figured that my dreams didn't have a world outside me. I guess I could dream up parents.

"Remember the new guy, the witch I told you about…" I started getting right to why I had really wanted to see him. His emerald eyes held mine waiting for me to go on. "He told me that I'm a witch. Can you believe that?" I asked expecting him to express the same outrage I'd felt.

"And you don't believe him?"

"Should I?" I retorted baffled.

He thoughtfully regarded me and said, "I can tell you want to believe, but I have always thought there was something unique about you."

"And if I don't want it?" I argued.

"Do you really have a choice if it is who you are? Do

you really want to deny such a powerful gift?"

"I don't know," I sighed more discouraged than before.

"I think you owe it to yourself to find out if that is who you are," he advised.

Maybe he had a point. What would it hurt to try? Maybe I owed it to myself and to Gavin. "You might be right," I conceded.

He put his arm around me in comfort, and I rested my head on his arm. "It doesn't have to change you as a person, if that is what you are worried about."

"How can it not?"

He brushed a piece of hair from my face. "Don't let it define you. You need to take control of the power if it is yours. It doesn't control you," his honey voice had softened.

Easier said than done, but I knew he was right. "Okay," I agreed. "It might be worth a shot."

His dark green eyes smiled at me, highlighted by the blond of his hair. "Brianna the witch – has a nice ring to it."

Reaching behind me I smacked him in the back of the head with my pillow, not missing this time. His laugh resounded off of my bedroom walls.

"You'll regret that Lukas Devine. Just wait…" I playfully threatened him.

"I'm looking forward to it," he replied.

Laying my head back on his shoulder I closed my eyes and was cloaked by his radiance. He brushed a light kiss on my forehead. When I opened them again, I was alone.

CHAPTER 24

BY THE THIRD DAY, I knew that I had to get up and face the truth. I couldn't hibernate in my room forever. My aunt was already worried sick about my state, and I didn't want to upset her further. Picking up my phone off the nightstand, I dismissed the gazillion text messages and missed calls. Tori, Austin, Sophie and Gavin had appeared to alternately contact me in some form. I figured it was only a matter of time before one of them thrust their presence upon me. And just because I may decide to resume my life in the real world, didn't mean I was exactly ready to talk with Gavin. I knew I couldn't avoid him indefinitely but tomorrow at school would be soon enough. If I was that lucky.

I think I had finally come to terms with my decision, not that I really had a choice. If I did indeed have magic, it wasn't just going to get up and walk away because I decided I didn't want it. From what I had already experienced it didn't work that way. It had already found ways to weave into my life without my knowledge. Accepting it and learning to control it seemed like the better solution.

What I planned on telling my aunt was another story. Right now when I wasn't even comfortable with the idea, probably wasn't the best time. For me it was better if I didn't tell her what I was or what I could possibly do. When the time came, if the time came, I would tackle it then.

My thoughts were interrupted by the ringing of my phone, and I was tempted to throw it across the room or flush it down the toilet. School must have gotten out and for three days I had been absent from class and from my friends.

Walking down the hall, I headed for the stairs to grab something substantial to eat. My appetite returned in a vengeance. Rounding the corner to the kitchen a voice startled me from behind. Pitching a scream worthy of breaking glass, a hand wrapped around my mouth stifling the shout of terror. His scent hit me all at once. Wild woods. I stopped struggling and relaxed in his arms. I seriously have had enough of people sneaking around in my house for one day.

"What are you doing here?" I screeched. My mind told me I should be mad at him for scaring the life out of me, but it had been too long since I had seen him. Turning to face him, my eyes ate him up. He was wearing all black and looked like he stepped out of an edgier Hollister ad. Hmm and smelled just as good. My heart jumped out of my chest for entirely different reasons than being frightened to death. I could be as angry or upset as I wanted to be, but it never changed the way my body reacted to him.

"I was worried about you. You haven't been to school in three days. You don't answer your phone. You don't text back. What am I suppose think?"

I don't know maybe that I wasn't ready to talk to anyone. "I needed some time." I opened the fridge and grabbed us something to drink, trying to still my overzealous heart. "How did you get in here?"

He raised his eyebrow. "You really think a locked door is going to keep me out? I was afraid you wouldn't see me," he answered taking a seat across from me at the table.

"You were probably right," I said popping the top on my coke.

"Bri, I truly never meant to hurt you," his eyes were filled with regret and pain. The sight tore at my heart. I had indirectly hurt him. "I only wanted to help. I know this is scary for you. When I saw you struggling with your control I knew I had to do something. If you let me and Sophie, we will help you any way that we can. I promise."

I propped my head on my hand. "I know. I was going to talk to you after school tomorrow. This whole witch thing is still… unreal to me," I confessed, letting the exasperation show.

"Let us show you what to do. We can figure it out together. I know Sophie would love to find out what you can do. She has been very difficult in your absence, not the easiest witch to deal with," he confessed.

I could only imagine. She was stubborn when she wanted to be.

"She's quite mad at me also, if that makes you feel any better," he added, leaning back against his chair, looking out of sorts.

"I'm not mad at you anymore. The shock has more or less worn off," I admitted. "To be honest, I am still not a hundred percent convinced I'm a witch, but I am willing to try. I need to know for sure one way or the other."

"Good, now I can tell Sophie to stop trying to hex me."

I gave him a half smile. "Not on my account."

He eyed me across the table with just a hint of a smirk. "She was so mad at me for what I did, she refused to talk to me the rest of the day, and then when she was speaking to me, she was yelling at me about what an idiot I was."

"She's such a good friend," I said taking a sip of my coke.

He snorted. "Lately I'd say your taste in friends is questionable. Look what you got yourself into." He smiled dangerously at me over the table.

"You're telling me," I agreed with him.

"Come over tomorrow after school?" he asked.

"I can't. I have work," I said, remembering that I needed to resume my responsibilities, which included my shift at the shop.

"Fine, the day after that," he suggested, slightly annoyed that I had to work.

"All right," I agreed.

"I'll pick you up after school."

I nodded my head. Witchcraft 101 here I come.

CHAPTER 25

WHEN GAVIN AND I ARRIVED at his house the following day, Sophie and Jared were waiting for us outside around back.

"This is going to be fun," Jared said all geared up. His dimples winked on either side of his cheeks mischievously. "Don't worry I'll go easy on you."

I rolled my eyes.

"You didn't think we were going to miss out on your first day of boot camp, did you?" Sophie asked smiling innocently.

Seeing Jared suddenly reminded me that I still didn't know what magic he could do. "Jared," I called bringing his attention to me instead of whatever joke he planned to prank. "Gavin promised me you would tell me what you can do," I informed him.

Jared's eyes twinkled, but it was Gavin's voice behind me who answered. "Not tell Jared, show her," he told him coming to stand next to me and taking my hand.

"I'd be delighted to," he was gleaming in roguery. His dimples winked on either side of his cheeks.

Right before my eyes Jared effortlessly began to

227

change. His form shifted so quick to the eye that I almost didn't believe – or see it. A gray and white coated wolf stood where Jared had been moments before, his eyes the same piercing blue as Gavin's. In a blink of an eye Jared had transformed into a beautiful fierce looking wolf.

I walked up to the wolf, needing to see for myself that he was indeed real. Kneeling to his level, I scratched the sides of his fluffy neck. His fur was much softer than I expected. Jared the wolf closed his eyes in appreciation at the neck rub.

At this point I was becoming good at weird. "Wow," I exclaimed. "You're a shiftshaper. That is seriously wicked. Any chance I'll be able to do that?" I asked standing back up.

Just as smoothly as before Jared returned to his human form. The three of them looked at me like I had grown horns. I think they had expected me to freak out or faint.

"You never fail to surprise me," Gavin commented. "Just when I think I understand you, you blindside me again. Why is it you don't bat an eye when Jared shifts, but you lock yourself away for days when I said you were witch?"

I eyed him levelly and shrugged. Even I don't understand how my mind works, why would I expect anyone else to. "Maybe I'm getting use to the unusual. I should since I am one."

"At least you're starting to believe," Sophie replied.

"Come on let's see what you can do," she said excitement brewing in her eyes.

"Where do we start?" I asked, having no idea what in the world I was supposed to be doing. This wasn't exactly like learning how to play battleship.

I sat across from Sophie on the grass. Jared and Gavin were behind us.

Sophie's started in a no BS voice, "Well, now that you are aware of the energy inside you it should be a little easier for you to focus on it. We need to get you to feel the energy so that you will be able to command it."

Okay sounded simple enough.

"Close your eyes," she instructed. I did as she said. "Now relax your breathing. Gavin says that your power is at its strongest when you are angry. I want you to find that energy source that feeds your anger. That is where we are going to pull your powers from. You need to be able to access it at your whim, not just when your emotions are out of control."

No longer did this sound simple as pie. "I don't know what I am looking for," I admitted feeling a little defeated.

"Just like your heart beats, magic has its own sound so to speak. For some it's a vibration, for others it's a humming, but it's there in your blood pumping alongside your heart. Once you recognize the source you can begin to tap into it," she explained. "I want you to listen, find the energy within you."

Listening I heard the rolling waves of the ocean, the evenness of my breathing, in and out. Focusing deeper on myself I picked up the stable rhythm of my heartbeats, pumping strong against my chest. And there keeping time with my heart was a steady hum, traveling throughout my body. I could follow its movements extending from one side to the other.

"I can feel it," I whispered to Sophie.

"Good," she said with a smile in her tone. "Now let's use it. Your powers seem to have an affinity with the elements according to what Gavin has seen. Concentrate on something from nature."

Something from nature. The first thing that came to mind was butterflies. I pictured the little soft pale yellow butterfly I sometimes saw hovering in the large tree outside my house. How its tiny wings sunbathed on the tree limbs during the summer. There was a little tingle at the base of my spine.

Biting my lip, I opened my eyes and saw nothing. "It didn't work," I said deflated. She could see the disappointment in my violet eyes.

"There won't always be so much preparation. Just like anything new the more you practice, the more in tune you will be with your powers." She looked above my head at Gavin and Jared. "You guys need to leave, you're distracting her. Especially you," she said pointedly to Gavin.

I could feel him smirking behind me, but neither protested as I heard them walk back inside the house. My cheeks bloomed in color at her insinuation. Groaning in frustration, I complained, "Why was it so simple before with Gavin?"

"Because you are fighting it. Before you didn't know what you could do. You opened yourself up on faith and trust, but you are unwilling to trust in yourself. It is holding you back. Believe," she told me.

Believe that I was a witch. Believe in myself. Take a leap of faith on myself. That was asking a lot. With a deep breath I closed my eyes again. Harboring all my determination and attention, I imagined the butterfly, except this time I multiplied by a dozen. Maybe if I envisioned more it would help boost my magic. Whenever I thought of spelling before, I thought of hocus pocus rhymes. I couldn't decide if this was harder or easier, harnessing the power this way.

The tingling I'd felt before tripled and expounded throughout my body, filling me with a heady feeling that I craved more of. My mind wanted to get swept away in the sensation.

"Brianna," I heard Sophie call my name. "Brianna!" It wasn't until the third or fourth time that her voice penetrated through my thickening concentration.

This time when I opened my eyes a whole new sight greeted me. Hundreds of butterflies in vibrant colors danced in the air around me. Purples, blues, turquoise, pinks. I've never seen such beautiful species before. Their delicate wings fluttering against my cheeks like tissue paper. Holding out my hand, a lilac one with black spots landed on the tip of my finger. Laughing I realized that magic didn't have to be scary, dark or unnatural, it could be wonderful.

I looked to the large picture window and saw Gavin grinning at me through the glass. His dark poetic features reflecting the excitement I felt. Turning to Sophie, she was staring at me.

"Holy crap. I didn't think I was going to be able to reach you," she said with butterflies in her hair.

"Did I do something wrong?" I asked, as they started to spread out.

"Are you kidding me?" she said smiling. "You just blew the roof off that spell. There must be two hundred butterflies. Very impressive. He was right," she commented. "I've never felt so much energy before and you weren't even at full potential."

My smile faded a little from my lips. It worried me each time one of them mentioned how theoretically strong my magic could be. I didn't want all that responsibility, and I didn't want to be different. Once in my life I wanted to be like everyone else, or in this case like other witches.

Gavin and Jared came back outside swatting at my butterflies.

"You're a natural," Jared stated, his dimples making an appearance.

"Great," I muttered.

Gavin must have noticed my change in spirit. He came to my side and whispered, "Let's go to my room. I think we've had enough witchery for one day."

I stared into his eyes, and then nodded. "Thanks Sophie," I called over my shoulder as we headed for the house. Most of the butterflies had taken off in flight.

"What's wrong?" he asked the moment we stepped into his room. It was just as I remembered and smelled just like him.

I sighed. "Everyone keeps telling me how much power I have. I don't want it all. I don't want to be some uber witch."

"I don't see how you have much choice in the matter."

"That's just it. I'm scared of it. What if I can't control it? You've told me that I've used it before, and I never even

233

knew."

"You used magic on me the first time we kissed," he revealed taking a step closer to me. The air suddenly charged with my aggravation and his aggression.

I don't know how that was supposed to make me feel better, because it didn't. If anything I felt worse. "What! What are you talking about?"

"I felt it that night, under the moon. You demanded me to kiss you. Your eyes lit with this incredible dark violet. The moon reflected in your sultry eyes."

"Are you saying I made you kiss me?" Dread wove in my belly at the anticipation of his answer.

"No… It wouldn't have worked if I hadn't wanted to. You just nudged what I was already wanting," he said backing me into a corner.

I ran a frustrated hand through my hair. Would everything in my life be so complicated? "I can't believe that I used magic to make you kiss me," I said in mortification, completely unaware that he had me cornered.

"You didn't *make* me Bri," he said, but I wasn't listening anymore.

"I'm sorry," I uttered and turned to leave.

He blocked my exit, grabbing onto my arm his fingers melted into my skin he was so hot. "I'm not," he said and then the world rocked on its axis.

He cupped the back of my head and brought his mouth down on mine. Before I even registered that his lips were on mine, there was a burst of heat everywhere.

My back hit the wall of his bedroom as he deepened the kiss, and I relished in his taste. Dark and delicious. The scent of him heightened every tiny blissful tingle. My world shattered.

Ravenously my fingers curled into his dark hair and yanked him closer. Too much space sat between us, and I couldn't get close enough. Even as the contours of his body molded against mine, it didn't satisfy the craving for him. I sank into his lips, basking on the feel of his silver hoop teasing mine. The undeniable urge to tug on it was almost too much to resist. I felt like I had this moment for eternity. This boy and the way he could make me feel, was beyond amazing.

It was paradise.

Moaning on an explosion of hunger, his hands roamed, skimming the sides of my breast. A shiver raced down my spine at the contact.

His mouth was just a breath away. "Tell me I didn't make you do that," I whispered.

"No, you didn't," he sighed. "I don't want to let you go," he confessed.

"Don't," I pleaded.

"I don't know that I have a choice," he admitted struggling with his emotions. "There is so much you don't understand... I don't understand."

"What more do you need to know? I thought my being a witch was what you wanted. Now you're telling me that you don't know what you want?" The mood was blown, and I was tired of feeling misplaced and disconcerted. I wasn't a yoyo.

"It's not that simple Bri," he argued.

"Nothing is with you. I think you should take me home," I stated emotionally spent.

CHAPTER 26

AFTER HE DROPPED ME OFF, I left his car without even a good-bye. Rushing inside I tiptoed up to my room. My aunt was home, and I didn't want to disturb her or honestly talk. I knew that if she took one look at me, she would see the raw emotions I couldn't hide. Closing the door softly behind me, the room was submerged in darkness. I reached for the light switch. Fumbling along the wall I must have miscalculated how far the switch was. Instead of my hand connecting with the switch as I expected, my head connected with the door of my bathroom.

Everything went black as I lost consciousness.

When I awoke I wasn't alone, and I was no longer in my room. There was giant size knot on the side of my head and a killer pounding at my temples. Scrambling to my feet off the blacktop I raised a hand to the side of my head and caught a flash of red take off around the corner.

"Hey," I yelled out after the figure.

Taking off, I hit the pavement at a dead run. Not exactly the smartest move. My head protested at the quick movements and slowed me down. As I turned the corner a woman with flaming hair and burning violet eyes so like mine stood a few feet in front of me. She smiled at me, and I couldn't help think she looked like an enchantress. And then it dawned on me. She was the woman from the painting in the Mason's library. What had Gavin said her name was?

Before I had the chance to mull it over, she beckoned me forward. I didn't really see how I had a choice. I had no idea how I got here, where I was, or what she wanted with me.

So of course I followed her.

As we walked I studied her, fascinated by her presence and the amount of confidence she oozed. Stunning in a black dress, her hair whipped out around her, a striking contrast to the dark she wore. I tore my gaze from hers and looked at my surroundings. It was past time I started figuring out what was going on, or at the very least where we were headed. As the shoreline came into view, I noticed the houses up on the embankment. We weren't far from Gavin's house and only a block or two from mine. Somewhere in the middle was my guess.

A gentle breeze ruffled my hair, and for the first time I looked down at myself and was stupefied to find that I wasn't wearing the jeans and tank top I had on all day. Instead I was donned in a white flowing dress that trailed behind me, a similar style to what the flaming haired woman wore. The top part cinched my waist in an old fashion corset. And I was barefoot.

Occasionally she looked over her shoulder at me to see if I was still following. Our identical eyes caught, and her name vibrated in my head.

Morgana le Fey.

Now I knew I hit my head a lot harder than I thought.

When we reached the shoreline, my feet sunk into the cool sand. The sky was dark and thickly layered in ominous clouds.

"What do you want?" I called to her back.

My feet were tired and beaten from the lack of protection. I didn't know how much longer I would be able to keep up with her. We were fighting against a wind that seemed to be getting stronger with each step, and I fleetingly wondered if I was the cause. Maybe I was heedlessly using my magic. Where my emotions were concerned anything was possible. What I did know was that my body wasn't up to this long trek after being knocked unconscious.

She never acknowledged my voice, but kept her steady grueling pace down the beach. I hadn't the slightest idea what I was doing out here in the middle of the night following a dead, and possibly fictional, woman. The more I thought on this the less smart it became. I wanted to deny the part of me that was pulled to follow her. I wanted to tell it to go to hell. My subconscious didn't care what I wanted, and I wasn't sure I could stop. I was beginning to think she had spelled me.

Continually we trudged across the beach with the wind picking up speed at our approach. There was a connection or tie to the air around me. I felt it in my core urging me to take control of it no matter that my body was exhausted and worn. Crossing my arms over my chest, I tucked them under refusing the pull.

Without the knowledge of my own powers and the ability to govern them, it was best to avoid using them. Even as I thought this, another part of me highly disagreed. It fought to surface and demanded to break free.

Stopping in her tracks, she turned to me, a troublesome grin on her blood red lips. Back facing the dark waters, her crimson hair and dark dress twirling with the winds. "Brianna my child, it is time for you to embrace your heritage," she said, her voice powerful. She threw out her arms, and the sky opened up in disorder at her command. Wow and I thought I had temperamental storm problems. She made me look like an amateur.

What did she mean heritage? I didn't have time to dwell on it because her magic flowed from her to the storm she started brewing. The electrifying energy of her spell cloaked around me and summoned mine to join her. The call was impossible to ignore as molten power flowed through my veins, I mimicked her movements, impervious to do anything else. Together our spell intertwined, and became so dominant and forceful I felt like we could easily destroy Holly Ridge with a flick of our finger. Nothing ever felt so wickedly good, like I was born for a purpose.

Throwing my head back, thunder cracked in the clouds and bolts of lightning struck. Her siren voice sounded in my head, encouraging me, not that I needed much motivation at this point. My magic recognized hers like they were long lost friends. Our spell blended harmoniously and effortlessly together as one.

"Born of my magic and blood, you shall be mine," she belted over the turning seas and howling winds.

With each word came a bolt force radiating my power. If there had been time to reflect on myself, I would have been frightened. Even as the richness of power engulfed me a tiny fraction in my mind sent a warning. Whispering to me, it sent Gavin's name to the forefront of my mind. I remembered him telling me how my moods often dictated the weather because I was insentiently using magic; weathercasting was what he called it. Glancing at the ferocious storm concocting, I knew that this wasn't me. It was just enough to break the hold the intoxicating spell had over me.

I didn't know what chance I had at getting out of here, but urgency insisted that I call for help in my single moment of sanity. He made a habit of saving me and was on the tip of my mind before I second guessed myself.

Gavin, I yelled over and over again.

Somehow I needed to wake from this nightmare, if it was indeed a dream. I prayed it was. My faith sank as nothing happened. No shift in the air. No fireflies. No Gavin. The energy I was projecting stumbled in my discouragement. Without him, I didn't know what hope I had of getting out of this perilous situation.

Why had I actually thought that would work?

Just when I was about to give up all hope, a shadowy form appeared higher on the bank, looking fierce, dangerous and pissed off. "Bri," he shouted.

Morgana whipped her head at his voice. He started to make his way towards me and dread spilled into my belly. I didn't want her attention focused on him.

"You cannot be here," she hissed displeased with Gavin's appearance. Her eyes darkened to a shade close to black, the deepest shade of purple.

Fear stabbed at my heart. All I could think was *not him*. If she hurt him because I brought him here, I would never be able to forgive myself. That much I was at least certain of.

Looks like I was going head-to-head with a bat-shit crazy witch.

Morgana shifted her energy at Gavin. I felt the alteration as our magic was no longer joined and without a second thought threw myself in its path. With a little help from my unpredictable magic, I made sure it was directed exactly to me.

The sheer force of it knocked me back ten feet, as I sailed like a doll in the air flattening me on my ass. It was worse than being hit with a bulldozer (well what I imagined being hit by a bulldozer felt like), all the breath was knocked out of me at the pressure of landing hard. Even with a softer surface like sand, it hit me solid and firm. Gasping for air, Gavin knelt down beside me, brushing the hair out of my face. His touch made me realize I was still alive. If he could make me feel fireflies at a time like this then I must not yet be dead.

"Silly girl," I heard her say. "He has no part in this." If I thought she was combustible before, this took being pissed to a new level – must be a witch thing. Her voice dripped with venom and spite.

Before she even finished her sentence I felt the draw of her magic. She had started the spell again. Winds so severe, they kicked up sand in our face. Visibility was out of the question as I lost sight of her. Deep out in the ocean a monster hurricane rose from the violent waters, groaning with sickening power. Spinning rapidly, the ugly twister headed for shore. With each passing minute, the whirlwind picked up speed, strength and ready to flatten anything in its path. Including us.

"Bri," Gavin called over the deafening winds, running his hands over my limbs, checking for injuries. "Wake up." He repeated again and again as this new threat grew closer to the shores. "You have to fight it and wake up," he screamed spitting wet sand.

"I don't know how," I admitted, my own voice sounding raspy and foreign.

"You do," he insisted. "Focus. Use your energy like you did today. Make yourself wake up."

He was right. I had to try. I had to save us. This was the only way I knew how. Doing as he instructed, I closed my eyes and searched for the flowing hum of energy. The crazy chaotic circumstances made it way more difficult to concentrate. Yet somehow I was able to find the thread I needed. Keeping every last bit of vigor on the only lifeline I had, the magic merged into my bloodstream, and I chanted, *Wake up! Wake up! Wake up!*

Afraid to open my eyes, I could no longer sense Gavin beside me. Collapsed on the shore, the white dress was plastered against me along with wet sand. Morgana's temptress laugh was ringing in my ears. Soaked to the bone, I laid on the beach too exhausted to move. A whizzing and whirling of wind caught some part of my mind that screamed danger. Opening my eyes I looked out into the turbulent waters and saw the murderous hurricane swirling out of control. My heartbeat started to burst from my chest as I realized the immediate threat barreling my way.

Morgana was nowhere in sight, her voice gone. All I could think about was the spell had not worked. I hadn't been able to wake myself from the nightmare or it was never a dream to begin with. I had failed.

Laying there on the beach I resigned my fate over to the hurricane that would surely sweep me away. Not an ounce of stamina remained in my body. Even the magic felt drained.

"Bri." Gavin's voice flittered from somewhere behind. He sounded like he was talking under water. "Bri," he called again. How appropriate that his voice would be the last I heard.

When his dark features appeared in my vision I thought I was hallucinating.

"Bri stay with me," he said like I had a choice. I didn't want to die, and I sure as hell didn't want him dying with me.

"Get out of here," I yelled, using the last strength I had, my voice gravelly.

The sapphire of his eyes radiated with magic as he

muttered a few hushed words. Silence erupted as the whizzing and whirling dissolved. I thought this is it. Now all I needed was the bright light.

He lifted me up into his arms. "I love you," I murmured against his neck and inhaled one last scent of the wild and recklessness that could only be him.

"Saving you is starting to become extremely dangerous and life-threatening. Way more than I bargained for," he said as he carried me in his arms. A moment later I blacked out again for the second time that night.

CHAPTER 27

DRIFTING IN AND OUT OF consciousness I awoke to bits and pieces of conversation around me. The voices all belong to one Mason or another. It seemed the whole family was in attendance, I could safely assume I was in their home.

"Is she going to be all right?" I heard Sophie ask. A cool damp cloth was placed over my forehead, as I became aware of the burning inside me.

"She has a good size bump on her head and is banged up some, but I think she will be fine. Her body and magic need time to recuperate. She needs rest, lots of it," Lily said. I felt her hand brush back my hair. Beads of perspiration gathered at the hairline.

"What are we going to tell her aunt?" Sophie asked.

"I don't know yet. Let's just see when she wakes up. Hopefully it will be soon," Lily replied.

The rest of the conversation was lost to me as I floated back into a deep sleep. A dreamless sleep. I was afraid now to close my eyes, but my body had other plans and didn't care for my fears.

There was no concept of time in my fitful sleep. I repeatedly woke, but didn't actually wakeup. I was more or less stuck in some in-between time warp of slumber. It was not exactly a journey I would like to take again.

"Is he okay?" I heard Lily ask in one of my lucid semi-conscious moments.

"Yeah. He is beating himself up about not being there for her sooner. He thinks he should have done something to prevent this," John replied, sounding strained.

I could only assume they were talking about Gavin. And that was just like him to think that he could have stopped this. Their voices trailed off as I went under yet again. The tittering between both worlds was depleting my energy. I couldn't fight it anymore and so I let it take me back to a place without hurt, feeling or terror.

When I emerged again, I was determined to stay awake this time. The seesawing was screwing with my mind, and I had to wake. I needed to get home before my aunt realized I was gone. My only hope was that time hadn't slipped away from me while my mind continued to plunge.

"She can dreamscape." I heard Gavin tell his parents.

"Are you sure?" John asked his son.

"Yes. It's how I knew where she was tonight. She's done it one other time before that I know of. The night we met."

Dreamscape? I hadn't the foggiest idea what he was

talking about. What had I done?

"Tell us what happened," John asked Gavin.

"I was sleeping when I heard her call my name. The next thing I knew I was outside in a wicked storm and Bri was standing on the shore in the middle of it all. I yelled out her name and that is when I noticed Morgana."

"Morgana was there? You are sure?" Lily asked. There was disbelief and bewilderment in her voice.

"Yes, it was her and she did not want me there."

"I don't doubt that. Would indefinitely mess up her plans I'd imagine," John said.

"What does she want with Bri?" he asked emulating my uncertainties.

"I don't know. But I doubt anything good can come from having the most powerful witch seeking you out in your dreams," Lily said.

Morgana the most powerful witch, echoed in my mind. Her power was unparalleled and yet I was certain that my magic felt so close to hers, like a twin. That couldn't be though, none of this made sense.

"How were you able to get her to wake up?" John asked.

"Morgana threw a spell at me and Bri stepped in its path. The force of it knocked her in the air like a rag doll. I was so scared." He sounded tired. "When I got to her side, she wasn't moving but was awake. I told her that she needed to use her energy and force herself to end the dream…and she did it. She found the strength to get us out of there." He struggled with keeping the aguish out of his voice.

I moaned as my head felt like it was split in half, the pain excruciating. Forcing my eyelids to open was like prying a can with my bare hands. The light casted in the room hit my eyes like a spotlight. Bubbles shaped themselves behind my eyes. Trying to lift my head proved to be a very bad idea. Spears of pain radiated from the sides off my skull. Moaning louder I brought my hand to my head and laid back on the pillow. Lily and Gavin were at my side instantly.

Lily lightly helped me lay softly back on the pillow. "Easy," she encouraged.

"Bri," Gavin breathed on a sigh of relief.

I groaned. Their voices so close to my hammering head, blasted pain to my temples. "Sorry," I squeaked. My own voice sounded scratchy and hoarse.

"Don't try and move too much. You need to rest your voice," Lily said filled with motherly concern.

I wasn't sure how much I could move, even if I wanted to. Everything felt bruised, battered and sore. "What happened?"

"How about we talk about it after you get better? I don't think you are in much shape to have the kind of conversation this would take," Lily suggested. "I've got to grab a few things." I watched her walk from the room.

"That complex, huh?" Like everything lately in my life it seemed.

Gavin smirked down at me, a strand of his dark hair falling over the eye with the silver bar. "What fun would it be without a little excitement and a dead witch haunting your dreams?" He sat down on the bed beside me and took my hand. "How are you feeling?"

I closed my eyes for a moment. "I've been better."

His expression flickered with a flash of anger.

"Don't," I croaked, my throat was so dry.

He handed me a glass of water and Lily came back into the room. She held a potion that I was sure was going to taste like bitter vinegar or worse. My facial expression must have given away my disgust.

She laughed lightly. "It's not as bad as it looks. I promise, and it will speed your healing time. That kind of trumps the taste."

She had me there. At this point anything to relieve the discomfort was a blessing. Helping me to a sitting position, she propped a mound of fluffy pillows behind my back. Wrinkling

my nose I gave the seaweed green mixture a look of
repugnance. My stomached turned just on sight, even though
the scent wasn't what I expected. The smell was a cross
between citrus limes and clover herbs. Not altogether bad, but I
wouldn't drink it voluntarily if it wasn't a matter of easing my
aches.

Taking a deep breath, I sucked it up and took a giant
gulp. Getting it down my throat was another matter entirely.
I've always had a sensitive gag reflex. Embarrassing myself
further was not an option, so I forced it down and was pleased
when it went smoothly.

"There you go dear," Lily coaxed. "Lie back down for
an hour or so and you will start to feel the effects." She
smoothed the hair that stuck to my face unflatteringly.

"What time is it? Will I be able to get home soon?" It
occurred to me that my aunt probably didn't know I was
missing, and if I could keep it that way, even better. I didn't
want her stressing about me any more than necessarily,
especially with all the responsibility she shouldered. The last
thing she needed was to think she had some out-of-control teen
on her hands. I'd been a model one so far.

"It's a little past one a.m. I think we'll be able to sneak
you home before morning," she said winking.

I smiled as best as I could in return and relaxed more

deeply on the pillows. She patted my cheek before leaving. Sophie replaced her at my bedside.

"Hey there," she said.

"Hey yourself," I managed.

A tear slipped from the side of her eye, she wiped it away with the back of her hand. "I'm sorry. I don't know why I'm crying... You really scared me tonight. When Gavin brought you inside –" Her voice stumbled on her tears.

"Sophie, I'm fine." I grabbed her hand. "I'm just a little weak, and my mind is fuzzy, stop worrying."

"I know. You're just the only real friend I have here," she said squeezing my hand.

"I'm glad we're friends." And it was true. I might not be the most popular or the friendliest, but I was close to the friends I had and was lucky to have Sophie as one of them.

True to Lily's words I started feeling better. Magic can hurt but it can also heal – quickly. Sophie lent me a change of clothes; the warm sweats made me feel like me again or as close as I could come to feeling normal. She gave me a long hug.

Gavin drove me home in his mom's car sometime in the wee hours of the morning. I felt better but was still so tired after the long night this was turning out to be. The picture of my own familiar bed sounded like heaven. I studied Gavin at the wheel and didn't know what I would have done if he hadn't been there tonight. If he wasn't here for this huge transformation my life was undergoing. I felt more connected to him than ever.

"About tonight –" I started before he cut me off.

"Don't say anything. This wasn't your fault."

"But it is," I insisted.

"Bri you are different, I've never met a witch like you. There is something about your energy and tonight I felt that same substance or whatever it is, in Morgana."

"What does that mean?"

"I don't know... yet. What I do know is that you need to rest. We can talk about this all later," he said as we pulled into my driveway. The sun was barely beginning to rise behind the house, framing the yard in a halo.

"Fine," I huffed. "I'm not dropping this."

He raised his eyebrow, knowing very well that this wasn't the last he'd hear of this conversation. "I never thought you were."

"How are we getting in?" I asked, yawning.

He smirked. "I got this."

Like I ever doubted him, when it came to breaking the rules, Gavin knew how to work it. I didn't ask what spell he was weaving, I really didn't want to know, just as long as my aunt didn't find out and wasn't hurt.

Walking into my bedroom was therapeutic in ways I never thought possible. Collapsing on the bed, Gavin came over beside me and tucked me in. He brushed the hair from my face and pressed a light kiss on my forehead. "See you tomorrow. Sweet dreams Bri," he whispered and a sparkling tingle of magic spread over my body.

CHAPTER 28

I GOT TO STAY HOME from school the next two days even though I was feeling much better. My aunt was hovering and beside herself over the fact that I was sick again. It wasn't like me; I was usually very healthy and had been as a child. These last few weeks with everything going on, put me on her radar, not a place I liked to be. But there was no way I could tell her what really happened, or that Gavin was a witch, let alone that I was a witch. I was too afraid to lose her.

Her opinion matters too much.

Gavin was at my door the moment my aunt left for the shop on the second day. He checked on me yesterday just like he said he would, though I spent more than half the day catching up on sleep, we never had a chance to really talk. Which was a blessing in disguise, because the more I had the chance to think over those nights events, the clearer I was that I had actually professed to loving him. He hadn't brought it up, and I wasn't about to. I knew in my heart that I loved him, but I wasn't yet ready to vocalize that love (except of course unless I was threatened with death). So making the mature decision, I decided to ignore whatever I said or thought I said. The events were still a little fuzzy.

"What are you doing here?" I asked opening the door.

Fireflies frolicked at the sight of him, an indicator I was on the mend.

"Checking up on you." He looked at me from head-to-toe, and it had anything but an unhealthy effect on me. I'd say my body was pretty much healed.

My cheeks flushed, and I cleared my throat. "Aren't you supposed to be in first period?"

"You're more important."

Flattered as I was, he needed to go to school, yet it didn't stop me from smiling. "That's crap. Go to school. I can't have you failing."

He smirked, toying with his hoop. "I won't, nothing a little magic can't fix."

I gave him a stern look.

"It's only one day Bri. I promise not to miss another day this…" he paused reconsidering what he was going to say. "Until winter break. Satisfied?"

"I guess." There was a meow from under his jacket. "Why are you meowing?"

He grinned and pulled out a fluffy black kitten. "Every witch needs a cat," he said, holding out a wriggling bundle of fur.

I couldn't help the cooing and ahhing this was, after all, the cutest kitten on the planet. I took the kitten from Gavin and holding him over my head I looked into his sweet baby eyes. "You are absolutely adorable." My heart tumbled for this itty-bitty little guy. I never owned a pet before, and I was sure that we were both in for a ride. I snuggled him into my arms and buried my face in his dark fur.

"I talked to your aunt first, and she said it was okay. I have a trunk full of stuff for him," he said watching me with amusement.

"He's perfect, but why the gift?"

"I told you, every witch needs one." His sapphire eyes sparkled. "Now… what are we going to name him?"

I was a little leery about his motives for giving me a gift.

"I was thinking Merlin," he suggested.

I scrunched me nose. "To obvious."

"You might be right, Gandalf?"

"That was a great movie," I said smiling "but I'm thinking something original." Petting his tiny head, I noticed a small white crescent shape on the back of his neck, the only white spot on him. "Lunar."

"Lunar," he said testing it out. Lunar let out the tiniest meow. "I guess he likes it." He scratched the top of Lunar's furry head and he purred on contact. The sound vibrated through his little body. "Oh I forgot. Your aunt asked me to pick up your homework assignments for you."

"And how did you manage that if you didn't go to school?"

"Do you really want to know?" His grin said that I definitely didn't want to know and no doubt, involved a spell with some form of deception.

I shook my head. "No, but I wished you'd spell it all finished."

"Already did."

"Gavin..." I groaned, giving him a look of steel.

"What? Your aunt just said to pick it up. She didn't say anything about you actually having to do it. Look, I was worried about you and your recovering. I didn't want you stressing and laboring over school work. You can't fault me for that."

I groaned. "You're impossible."

"So my parents tell me," he said, but not like he really was offended by it. "How are you feeling?" he asked the mood changing in his eyes. Concern replaced the light banter.

Sitting on the couch I placed the kitten in my lap. "I'm fine. Stop asking." I stroked Lunar's back as he tried to attack my fingers with his baby paws.

He sat down next to me, the couch sinking with his weight. "You look much better," he said.

"I am," I insisted. "In fact I'm going back to school tomorrow. Oh tell your mom I said thank you again. What she did for me saved me a lot of trouble."

"She was glad to do it, but you know Bri that you are going to have to tell your aunt sometime," he stressed. Another topic I wasn't comfortable yet dealing with. At the rate my list of uncomfortable topics was growing, I was going to be swimming over my head in problems.

I shifted my eyes back down to a wiggling Lunar. "I know," I admitted softly.

"When you're ready... I'll be there to help you."

Lifting my eyes back to his I replied, "Thanks, it means a lot having you here."

"You mean a lot to me," he admitted in that husky tone. My heart swelled, thumping wildly.

We hung the rest of the day on the couch watching TV and just relaxing. He left right around the time school was due out. I walked him to the door.

He trailed a finger along my cheek, lifting my chin with his finger. His touch was soft and electric. I leaned into his caress, my eyes sparkling with out-of-control awareness. I was afraid to think about kissing him, who knew if I would accidently spell him, but none of that stopped my body from moving closer to his. My mind or magic had little control over that. He bit on his silver hoop as his head lowered fraction by fraction to mine. I held my breath as I waited impatiently for his lips.

Lunar meowed between the two us, breaking the spell, and I internally moaned inanely at the lost kiss. He was smashed between us, looking up at me with those baby blue eyes.

"I'm picking you up tomorrow morning for school," he said in a gruff voice.

I hoped he was as affected and would suffer as much as I would without those few minutes of bliss that I would indubitably be thinking about. There was an aggressive part of me that just wanted to grab ahold of him and lay one right on that silver hoop teasing me.

Swallowing the lump in my throat, I nodded my head. "Bye."

Closing the door wistfully behind, I plopped myself down on the couch. I knew everyone was worried about my health. After two days I was going stir crazy. Deciding I needed to get out of the house, I thought a small trip to the Riverfront Farmers Market for dinner tonight would be nice. My aunt was having one of the other girls close so she could be home early to supposedly take care of me. She was really worried.

There was still plenty of time left in the day to get there, shop around and make it back to start dinner before my aunt was due home. I loved the farmers market in Wilmington, and the idea was too much to resist. They had more than just the average fresh produce. There were vendors for just about everything from jewelry, arts, crafts to musical entertainment and every kind of fruit, vegetable and herb you could imagine. Plus the fresh air would do me good.

I twirled the moonstone and amethyst necklace at my neck rolling the idea in my head and while patting Lunar with the other hand. He was curled up next to me taking a nap feeling pretty smug. Decision was easy, I had to get out of this house, and I'd deal with any backlash later.

Picking up a protesting Lunar I placed him on my bed near where his food and litter sat in my bathroom. With him being so tiny I was afraid to let him wander the house by himself. I was tempted to bring the troublemaker with me; he was going to be a handful.

After shutting him in my room I grabbed my keys and headed for Wilmington.

The drive was easy and one I'd done a million times before. During the trip, Tori and Austin had each sent me a text on their way home asking how I was doing. I missed them and was ready to get back to my *normal* routine. When I got to

Wilmington the sun was shining, the sky was crystal blue, and I soaked up the rays after being cooped up in my house. Strolling leisurely from vendor to vendor looking at all the merchandise my mind wandered. I had a deep reflection mood going. I wanted to just enjoy the drama free day, lose myself in the crowds and my own head.

My world might never be the same. Who I am had changed. Magic was a part of my life, and I needed to find a way to conquer the power inside before it destroyed me or hurt someone I loved. Unearthing answers to questions of the past and the future seemed like my best hope at figuring out what was happening to me.

I don't know where Gavin and I stood or why he was reluctant to take what we had, further. But I know my heart and what I feel for him won't diminish, something twined us together like vines to a trellis. How could it when my entire being was bursting with love for him. My only hope was that he would someday return that love.

I hadn't decided what to tell my two best friends about my new found magical powers. I don't even know if I should. This would be a gigantic secret to hide from them, and I don't know how long I'd be able to keep up the charade. I could always spell them. Well not really.

It was impossible to believe all that has happened and

my senior year had barely begun. I didn't have a clue what I was doing after high school let alone next week. Winter was coming upon us as the last few days of fall started to fade.

Fingering the intricate design on a hand woven bracelet, I looked up and caught a flash of sandy hair reminding me of Lukas. Squinting I tried to see his face, because the similarities were frighteningly familiar, and I've had enough fright lately. The boy angled his face towards me, grinning at the girl behind the table. Lacking Lukas's lustrous smile, I breathed again, my eyes deceiving me.

Deciding that I'd had enough fresh air for the day, I sped up my shopping and headed directly to the produce. Picking through a stack of cumbers, I selected a few and moved on to the green and yellow peppers. Rifling in the peppers I was suddenly saturated with an acquainted energy. Lifting my violet eyes over the stack of vegetables, I searched for the source. Difficult with the number of people about, plus I really didn't know what I was looking for.

Then across the booth from where I stood, emerald eyes smiled at me from over the fresh produce stand. This time I knew I wasn't dreaming, and my eyes weren't deceiving me.

"Lukas?"

To be continued…

BONUS MATERIAL:

Yummy

Scenes from Gavin's point-of-view

~The Run-in~

This godforsaken town had the damnedest weather. Ducking under the overhang on the side of the brick building, I shook the water from my dark hair. It was soaking wet from a storm that just appeared out of nowhere, pouring like buckets and lighting the sky up like the Fourth of July.

My first day of school, and I already couldn't wait to get the hell out of here. So much so that I skipped out on over half of my classes, I felt so out of place. Not one other person from what I could tell, was like me. In Chicago, I wasn't such a freak. Here I felt like I stuck out like a sore thumb.

Sometimes being a witch wasn't all that it was cracked up to be. Usually it just kicked ass. Today it just sucked.

Leaning against the worn red bricks, I took a deep breath of the rain damped air. If I hadn't been so down in the dumps and pissed off about the move, I would have recognized the storm for what it was – a surge of power.

As it was though, I didn't realize it until after I had an armful of a very nice surprise.

From where I was hidden, I saw her turn the corner in haste and I thought *great there goes my solitude.* Hopefully she wouldn't bust me for ditching, but I figured I was safe since it seemed like she was running from something.

A second later she practically ran into my arms.

Instinctually I brought my hands up to steady her, and kept us both from hitting the ground. In the moment that our skin connected, a gush of electricity poured over me. More intense then I had ever felt from another witch. And I knew instantly what she was.

A witch.

And an extremely powerful witch by the shock she'd dealt me. It was astonishing and fierce. Stunned, I couldn't believe that this po-dunk town had such a witch. What was she doing living in Holly Ridge?

Looking down, all I saw was a waterfall of dark hair. She was small, only coming up to the top of my chin and fit perfectly against me. Lifting her head from my chest, she peered up at me from under long, thick black lashes.

She stole my breath.

Her eyes.

Her eyes had the afterglow of magic. God they were stellar.

Bright.

Crystal.

Like the finest cut amethyst.

She gaped at me, and I couldn't help but be pleased. At least I wasn't the only one whose jaw just about dropped to the ground. She was that gorgeous. My eyes sparkled as she continued to stare at me, and I lifted a brow.

Entranced, I watched her eyes move over each part of my face. When those enchanting eyes landed on my mouth I couldn't help the smirk. She didn't have the first clue what her thorough inspection was doing to me.

Hell, after all I am a guy. A teenage guy at that. Did she think she could look at me like that and I wouldn't be affected? I wasn't made of stone.

Apparently neither was she. Her eyes darkened, and my pulse jumped. Leaning in, I could smell the strawberry gloss on her lips.

Bliss.

I wanted very much to taste those lips right now.

Would they be as soft as they looked?

Would she taste like strawberries?

Most importantly, would she kiss me back?

This was a very nice treat I hadn't expected to tumble into. Very nice indeed.

Running my thumb gently down her arm, she

shuddered in my arms. Whatever spell had been between us, she broke it, stiffening in my embrace. And I was filled with disappointment. I didn't want to let go just yet.

"What are you doing?" she demanded, her voice rough.

Someone just got her panties in a bunch. I lifted an eye at her tone. "Saving you it seems. Obviously I'm not the only one ditching last period."

Smooth man. Way to call her out.

She took a step back, and I regretted the words immediately. Her eyes roamed over the rest of me causing my body to long for the contact of hers again. She made my blood boil with just her eyes.

"I – I don't normally ditch class," she stuttered cutely, running a hand through her dark hair.

I enjoyed the sound of her frazzled voice, and shrugged my shoulders.

She narrowed her gaze at me. "I've never seen you before. Do you even go here?" she asked.

"Umm yeah – it's my first day," I admitted smirking, unable to help myself.

"You ditched on your first day?" she asked like she couldn't fathom the idea, but here she was with me, ditching class.

"Sure. It seems worth it now," I said shoving both

hands in my pockets. They itched to touch her again. "I'm Gavin." I had hoped by giving her my name, I would get hers.

And I wasn't disappointed. "Brianna," she replied right before the last period bell rang, sounding the beginning of ninth period. Her eyes got wide at the sound. "I should go," she mumbled.

I leaned back against the wall studying her. Not once did she let on that she knew what I was. It puzzled me to say the least. "I'll be seeing you Bri."

She mumbled an apology, and then fled to the parking lot. A part of me wanted to go after her. There was so much I wanted to know, to ask her. But I just let her go.

There was always tomorrow, I thought smirking.

Holly Ridge just might not be such a death sentence after all. Things just got a whole lot more intriguing. I never would have thought I'd look forward to going to school.

~The kiss~

I watched as the array of emotions flickered over her face. She had for the first time believed in herself. Believed in her magic and the result had been astonishing. The sudden change in her violet eyes tugged on my heart. Would I always feel this overwhelming need to protect her? Even from the simplest of things?

"What's wrong?" I asked the moment the door to my room was closed. Her eyes looked around the room before settling back to me. She had the most incredible eyes. There was still a glimmer of magic shimmering in them.

She sighed. "Everyone keeps telling me how much power I have. I don't want it all. I don't want to be some super witch."

It pained me to hear the anguish in her voice, and the struggle she was going through learning to wield her powers. I didn't have the command to change her fate, and I was selfish enough that I was glad we had this in common. It not only connected us, but there was something else between us that I couldn't even explain.

What she needed to hear was the cold truth, some tough love. Nothing would be gained by pretending ignorance. It wouldn't make her power less or more. "I don't see how you have much choice in the matter," I replied.

"That's just it. I'm scared of it. What if I can't control it? You've told me that I've used it before, and I never even knew." Her eyes were wide and brimming with uncertainty, doubt.

Immediately I thought about the night we'd first kissed. Though her fears were all warranted, she didn't give herself enough credit. She was so much stronger. I could feel the strength of her power pulsing from her, even if she couldn't. It washed over me.

I took a stepped towards her, the ribbon of my magic calling to hers, pulling me to her. The admission was tumbling from me before I even had a chance to think about. "You used magic on me the first time we kissed."

"What! What are you talking about?" she asked puzzled, and her amethyst eyes darkened.

It made my blood rush. She didn't have the foggiest idea how those eyes got to me. All I knew was there was too much space between us. "I felt it that night, under the moon. You demanded me to kiss you. Your eyes lit with this incredible dark violet. The moon reflected in your sultry eyes."

"Are you saying I made you kiss me?" Her voice horrified.

This was coming out all wrong. How was I blundering so horribly bad?

It was turning into an epic fail.

"No…" I pleaded for her to understand. "It wouldn't have worked if I hadn't wanted to. You just nudged what I was already wanting," I said advancing on her ending up in a corner.

She sifted her fingers through her hair, and the scent of her shampoo hit me in the gut. "I can't believe that I used magic to make you kiss me," she replied with her cheeks tinting pink.

The flush of color was endearing. She was too occupied to notice the gleam in my glance. "You didn't *make* me Bri," I reiterated. I didn't know how else to make her understand what I was so miserably bombing at trying to explain. There was something between us that was undeniable.

"I'm sorry," she uttered and attempted to leave.

I blocked her exit, and wrapped my fingers around her arm. An electrified bolt zinged on contact, a result of our magic fusing together. I watched as her eyes shot tiny purple stars. "I'm not," I demanded and promptly brought my lips down on hers.

Our mouths melding together, she tasted inexplicably like the sweetest strawberries. Her back hit the wall as I pulled her closer so our bodies meshed. I was done trying to hide from what she made me feel, done ignoring that there was something larger between us than just being witches. It was past time I stopped pretending she was *just* a girl. Every fiber in my being knew Bri would never be *just* a girl.

Her fingers curled in my hair, and her teeth scraped

over the hoop on my lip. The world exploded behind my eyes. I felt her heart beating wildly like a train against mine. Trailing a hand up and down her side, my fingers seemed to have a mind of their own, and I was unable to resist the temptation.

Good God. She made everything disappear, everything except her.

She pulled back just a fraction. It was all I would really allow, and I stifled a whimper. "Tell me I didn't make you do that," she murmured against my mouth. It was nearly impossible to not take her lips again.

I sighed, knowing that if I didn't pull away now, I wouldn't be able to. This moment, this time when she was confused and unsure wasn't right. "No, you didn't," I assured. "I don't want to let you go." At least that was the truth.

"Don't," she pleaded.

Heaven help me, she was killing me. Literally killing me. I wasn't about to take advantage of her no matter what my body encouraged. She didn't need another complication in her life, and I still didn't know exactly what was going on. All I knew was that there was so much more to Bri than either of us could possible know. "I don't know that I have a choice," I said regretfully. "There is so much you don't understand... I don't understand."

"What more do you need to know? I thought me being

274

a witch was what you wanted. Now you're telling me that you don't know what you want?"

"It's not that simple Bri," I argued.

"Nothing is with you," she said flatly.

CPSIA information can be obtained at www.ICGtesting.com
Printed in the USA
BVOW08s2237090815

412549BV00001B/68/P